stagecoach

stagecoach

benjie willow the orphan series
book two

Ash Lingam

WISE WOLF
BOOKS

WISE WOLF BOOKS
An Imprint of Wolfpack Publishing
wisewolfbooks.com
1707 E. Diana Street
Tampa, FL 33610

Paperback ISBN 978-1-965596-50-0
eBook ISBN 978-1-965596-10-4

Benji Willow is dedicated to a boy I once knew long ago.

You can take the boy out of the country but you can never take the country out of the boy.

Arthur Baer

stagecoach

one
gold fever

I didn't know if I was hearing things in my dreams or if I was half awake. It sounded like someone was speaking. As the words slowly distanced themselves, I drifted back into a more profound state of slumber. I heard somebody talking again a moment later, and a pale light shone behind my eyelids. All I wanted was for them to go away so I could finish my pleasant dream. I was happy where I lay.

"Benji, wake up," Chito-Ochi said, shaking my shoulder. "It's time to go. You don't want to be late and miss your ride, do you?"

"Go? Miss my ride?" I pushed myself up, sitting in my bunk and using my fists to rub away the sleep. I blinked and asked, swinging my bare feet to the floor, "Where're we going?"

"Malvo said it's time to get back to work. I think he is already bored. It looks like we are going for a ride. It is about time we did something other than sit around. I have been lazy and getting fat."

"Don't you think it's a little too soon? Malvo still hasn't gained back all his weight and strength. His mind is fine, and I know he seems all right after the fall, but he's skinnier than before—he's also lost a lot of muscle. He doesn't seem as big as he did."

"Maybe you are getting bigger, and we are the same. What you and I think about Malvo Tanner has little to do with things," Chito-Ochi replied, grinning. "He is the one who must know when he is ready, not us. We are going to be riding on a stagecoach, anyway. That will make it easier, at least for him. For us, not so much. We will be with the driver in the hot Texas sun all day up on the top. We're their shotgun guards."

"I've never been on a stagecoach. Heck, I've never even seen the inside of one. The only thing I've ridden besides a horse was a buckboard wagon, which was all the way down the Chisholm Trail with my folks—something I wouldn't want to do again."

"Soon, you will see one up close, but you will be too busy to enjoy the ride. Malvo has signed us up to work as security, so you and I must ride on top."

"Why would they want so many guards? I thought there was usually only one plus the reinsman."

"This stagecoach will be carrying a strong box full of silver," the Choctaw Indian replied. "It is about time we did something. For every pound Malvo lost, I gained two. It is time for action before I get fat and lazy. Malvo and I know the bullwhacker driving the stagecoach, but he will have his hands full if we have trouble, so we can't count on him if bandits strike."

"So, you and I are gonna ride on the top? That sounds like fun more than like work."

Chito-Ochi chuckled. "It's nice on the roof. You get to see everything as we pass by, unlike those inside. They usually ride with the curtains closed to keep the dust out and do not see a thing. Plus, with the carriage closed, it feels like a sweatbox. That's where Malvo will be. He is going to act like an ordinary passenger. Hopefully, he won't be recognized. Lucky for him, most of our enemies think he is dead. They won't be expecting him. If bandits are on the trail, they will think there are only two guards: you and me. It will give us an edge if we have problems."

"Lately, trouble seems to follow me around like a shadow. I've probably seen enough desert, too, but it'll be nice to get back to work. I was wondering if I would ever find another job. Lucky for me, it turned out I never lost the one I had."

"Don't worry about Sheriff Boon Cassidy. You ended your time with him honorably. He knew if Malvo got better, he would want you back, and even though the sheriff is mean and has a dangerous reputation, he's still no match for Tanner. Let me tell you a little secret. Most of the men the sheriff shot he bushwhacked, but they also deserved to die. It is important that El Paso has a lawman like him, or the town would go wild like it was before. Back then, it was dangerous to walk down the street."

When we reached the Butterfield Overland Stage Company office, an empty coach waited idly out front, and a six-horse team stood nearby, shifting their hooves as they were rigged up. A chalkboard on the front of the building said El Paso, Independence, La Grange, Bastrop, Austin, New Braunfels, and a couple of others. The last stop was San Antonio.

I recognized that it was our destination. I knew it was a big city of over twelve thousand people. From the beginning of the Civil War, it grew to over eight thousand people, many suffering from the effects of the vicious war between the North and the South. I couldn't even imagine that many people in one place. I wondered what the towns in between were like.

The original source of the stagecoach line was San Francisco, and it ran all the way to St. Louis, Missouri. That was a total of two thousand seven hundred ninety-five miles. That meant twenty-five days of hard riding with dozens of stops to change teams along the way. They could rig new horses, grease the wagon's axles and be underway in less than ten minutes at the lay-way stations. You'd better travel as swiftly as possible when carrying silver through places like Texas.

"It is five hundred fifty miles of fair road to San Antonio but it's also known as a main route for bandits," Chito-Ochi said. "The driver, Jimmy 'The Whip' Johnson, said we should be there in four days if we run ten hours a day, only stopping a few minutes to change teams."

"I don't care what we've gotta do. Anything is better than working for Sheriff Cassidy. I must say that I feel much safer with you and Malvo. I figure that

Boon would eventually shoot me, too—especially when he's blind drunk. When he goes on a binge, I doubt it matters to him who he shoots."

The Whip walked the horses to his rig, grabbing the reins close to the bit rings, and led them to the wagon tongue, fastening them to the coach. Once the team was hooked up, he glanced at his tarnished pocket watch. Suddenly, the door of the stage company burst open, and seven people stumbled out, racing for the best seats.

Everybody wanted to sit by the window even though the leather curtains would remain closed to keep the dust out. Malvo was the last to walk out the door, but he ignored us and the driver, who he also knew. He acted like he had never seen us before.

"It's a hell of a four-day journey to San Antonio, and we run from first light until we see fireflies in the coming night," Jimmy The Whip said. "We only stop for meals and change the team of horses. That gives you fifteen minutes to eat. The passengers get thirty."

"We better quit wasting time then," Chito-Ochi said. "Climb up the wheel spokes and hub to the driver's box, then use the seat to climb onto the stage's roof. You can leave your personal possessions in the front boot under the driver's seat."

Six men were present, and two of them had wives with them. Everybody but the women were visibly armed, and they probably had señorita pistols in their purses. Nobody walked the streets of El Paso without a gun of some sort. Gunfights and shootouts were common enough for the townsfolk to always be prepared.

The stage's braces groaned when the passengers climbed aboard. The horses got nervous, but the driver booted the brakes and wrapped the reins around the beam. A short, white-haired man sat in the driver's box, grinning like a fox. His smile showed a mouth full of gums and no teeth. He kept his hand-carved false wooden teeth in his vest pocket for eating. Still, mischief and life twinkled in his light blue eyes. Mad-Dog Reed's face was wrinkled like an old dog.

Chito-Oche walked to the stage door and slammed it shut with a bang. "Jimmy says you should keep the leather curtains down if you don't want to choke on the dust."

As soon as the driver shouted, "All aboard!" Jimmy yelled as he cracked a bullwhip over his head, then looked at us and nodded. The horses strained at the reins as the driver looked down. "Come on, you two. We don't have all day. As soon as the last passenger's feet leave the ground, we're gonna be underway. Hold on to your hats, ladies and gentlemen. I'm afraid we're in a hurry to get to San Antonio, so it's gonna be a rocky ride."

At the last minute, a man came running down the street with a large pouch in his hands. On the side, it said Overland Mail Company.

"Sorry, I'm late, Jimmy. It won't happen again."

"Your boss would have your hide if you haven't made it, boy. The mail is supposed to run on time. It's lucky for you that we're running five minutes late."

No sooner did I sit down and grab ahold of the straps across the strong box than the stage jerked into motion. We rumbled down the street in seconds as the wagon wheels corkscrewed dust, leaving a growing cloud in our wake as it quickly gained speed. As we raced through town, the pedestrians caught in the middle had to dive for cover to keep from getting run over. I never knew a stagecoach could move so fast.

I had to hold on for dear life to avoid getting thrown off. Jimmy's driver didn't seem to notice the pedestrians he nearly ran over, or if he did, he didn't seem to care. He believed that the stage, money, and mail all had to run on a strict time schedule, and everybody in town knew that when the stage rolled out, you had better get out of the way. Right then, the bull-whacker was focused on getting the rig rolling faster.

Chito-Ochi seemed to maintain a delicate balance and never wavered despite the erratic movement of the coach. The driver appeared to be part of the rig and horses as he effortlessly moved in rhythm with the coach. He had obviously been doing this all his life. The steel-wrapped wooden wheels blurred, and the coach slid when Whip took a corner at excessive speed. Two wheels momentarily left the ground as the back broke traction and slid around the corner, only for the driver to crack the whip again urging the horses to race faster. I was nearly thrown off the top. I knew I had better learn to move with the stage's motion or risk getting thrown off.

Even though it was dangerous, I enjoyed every exciting moment. I had never gone so fast, and I loved

it. I looked over at my Choctaw friend, who was smil-
ing, too. Now, I didn't envy Malvo inside the coach at
all. Once we hit the edge of town, the old driver let it
rip, and we raced across the countryside as my hair
tickled my ears under my hat. I had to slap my hand on
the crown to keep it from blowing off as my long hair
fluttered.

Chito-Ochi's pigtails blew horizontally in the wind
created by the racing stage. It seemed like it was on the
verge of going out of control, but I felt Jimmy knew
what he was doing. His confident face told the story. I
briefly wondered what it would be like inside. I didn't
think I would care to change. I imagined the women
feeling sick. How about the smell? I liked it just fine on
the roof with Chito-Ochi out in the fresh morning air.

Several teepees stood in the distance, surrounded by
numerous Indian ponies. Their black silhouetted
figures wander, grazing around the camp. They didn't
even look when our stage roared down the road. They
had to have seen us with a twenty-foot-tall brown cloud
chasing behind. I stared across the wide-stretching
plains and at the mountains on the other side. Near
midday, I saw antelope bounding across the hillside,
and on a faraway ridge, I saw shadows standing long
beside a pack of coyotes as they followed each other
head to tail.

The stage moved under me like I was riding a
bucking bronco. At first, I had to hold on for dear life,
but after a couple of hours, I got the coach's rhythm by
watching Johnny. He rode along like an experienced
fisherman on roaring sea in force ten gale winds. His

head hardly moved as he anchored himself into the seat with his heels against the front boot. Somehow, he managed to keep ahold of the reins while swinging the whip in large circles and cracking it over the horses' heads.

The country climbed deep brown mountains scattered with cedar elms, bur oaks, and Chinese pastiches on the mountainsides. In between, it was covered in prickly pear, claret cup, and rainbow cactus. It was already so hot and humid that I pulled at my shirt, which was stuck to my body. The overhead sun pushed more heat onto the plains.

I removed my cover and raked my fingers through my dripping wet hair and down my young, beardless face. I slipped my hat back on and passed my shirt sleeve across my forehead, finally pulling the brim low over my eyes.

We passed a field of dazzling yellow sunflowers; their faces dished toward the sun. They were as tall as horses' backs. Everything around him seemed so large that it was hard to judge distances. Landmarks that appeared nearby took a long time to reach.

The driver, Chito-Ochi, and I saw it just before we hit, but nobody was ready for the impact. Still, we knew exactly what would happen, and we braced ourselves. Barely visible across the trail were woven thatch mats covered with dust to hide a narrow but deep trench across the width of the weathered road. It was small enough to effectively disguise but big enough to disrupt the function of the stage abruptly. I knew it would bring us to a jolting halt, so I braced myself as best I could and held onto the metal railing around the luggage rack.

It buckled the first two horses' legs as soon as they hit the ditch and sent them sliding on their chests, screaming in pain. Then four more followed as the inertia-maintained motion, and they continued to slide as one. Halfway to a stop, they tangled legs and rolled, breaking two of the horses' limbs. The others screamed, trying to free themselves from their harnesses.

Someone had carefully planned this out, and they'll show up any second.

When the front wheels of the stage hit the trench, it flipped completely over, tumbling in the air before landing on its side. Chito-Ochi flew like a bird, somehow maintaining his balance, and landed like a cat on all fours not far from the broken coach. I was tossed high into the air, my arms flailing as though I was trying to fly. Everything was happening so fast; it hadn't all sunk in yet, but I knew we were getting robbed.

Since I weighed a fraction of Chito-Ochi, I got thrown twenty feet into the air. When I landed in the tree's bough, I heard limbs cracking under me, but the sound got lost in the noise of horses screaming as the sliding stage nearly ground to a stop on its top. Everybody inside got tossed around like rag dolls until it finally screeched to an alarming halt and rolled onto one side. Luggage was scattered to the wind, and the women inside the cabin found their dresses over their heads, showing their petticoats. I peered at them hidden in the tree.

I wonder what Malvo is going to do. I hoped they

don't kill Chito-Ochi outright. I wrapped my fingers around the walnut grip of my father's Colt Walker. It was a miracle it was still in my holster, but my Winchester was lying beside the broken stage. The sun glinted off the polished metal.

Then I saw what we were up against. They were thin-lipped, sun-darkened men in range clothes and dark leather chaps. All four had colorful large bandanas tied around their necks. Each had a revolver in his hand and fought with his horse's reins with the other. The animals were spooked by all the noise from the crashing stagecoach.

Chito-Ochi stood as still as a stone, waiting to see what happened next. He had one hand on his gun and the other on his Bowie knife. I could see Jimmy "The Whip" Johnson lying on the ground, grumbling. White bone contrasted against his sunburned skin. A jagged hole showed a gaping wound on his broken arm. The blood drained from his face as the pain hit.

As the passengers tumbled out, nobody looked up. I continued to hide in the dense foliage, afraid to take a peep. Luckily, I didn't weigh much and got tossed into the air like a bag of feathers. Finally, when my breathing settled, and I got my balance, I parted the branches before me and sneaked a peek. Chito-Ochi quickly glanced up, and our eyes locked. He frowned, and he quickly turned away. He didn't want the outlaws to see me.

To draw the thieves' attention off me, my Choctaw friend began to dance and sing what I guessed was his death song. He didn't have any doubts about White men's desire to kill Indians. He had the Comanche to thank for that. I suddenly realized what might happen to my new friend. I ducked deeper into the branches full of leaves hidden from below as I prayed to God that they wouldn't look up.

All four outlaws rushed to the wagon, and in seconds, the stage, driver, guards, and passengers were captured. Incredibly, I was the only one who remained free. I stared at Malvo, and it was as though he could feel my gaze.

"Malvo," I mouthed the word in barely a whisper.

The barrel-chested Tanner snapped his head in my direction as soon as he heard my voice, but his eyes said it all. I clamped my mouth tight and hardly breathed as I backed farther into the cover of the oak tree. Its dense leaves kept my face and body hidden. I could feel the limb beneath me swaying in the stiff breeze.

"Get the strongbox off the top and shoot off the lock. And make sure it doesn't ricochet off and kill somebody." He tossed his man two pairs of saddlebags. "Put the money in there."

The three men climbed down from their horses and did as they were told. The strongbox had broken free and twisted out of shape, but the lock held. Suddenly, a gunshot rang out, and instantly after, the shooter yelled. Part of the lock had broken loose from the blast of the bullet had nicked his cheek. He held his hand to his face, and it came away bloody.

"Stop your gawking and finish the job. It's no more than a scratch."

They look like shootists to me, I thought. *I hope they*

take the money and let us go. Something else suddenly crossed my mind. *I'm alone again, this time in the wildest country in West Texas.*

"Is that you in there, Malvo Tanner? I see your Choctaw friend is here, so I reckon you won't be far. I'll give you to the count of ten before I shoot the Indian."

As the people on the stage struggled to untangle themselves, somebody pushed the door up and open. The first one to scamper out was a young lady in fancy dress. Now, the sky-blue material was smudged with dirt, sweat, and blood, but it didn't appear to be hers.

"Is that you out there, Henry Crowder? Are you working for that traitor and liar, Sheriff William Egan? What's he done?"

"He's put a bounty on your head and the Indian's too. All I have to do is get you to San Antonio in one piece."

"Why, I was headed for San Antonio, anyway. Why didn't you wait? Now you've got to lug us across five hundred miles. And I was just about to fall asleep."

The next head that popped out was a man wearing a leather eyepatch and an empty sleeve pinned at the elbow. Malvo lost his left arm in the Battle of Sharpsburg—better than the twenty-two thousand who lost their lives in the clash. One of the cowboys rode up with his paint's reins in his fist. Another brought the four horses from the stage that survived. Gunshot ran out, killing the two with broken legs. Our horses were on stringlines at the back but were far enough away from the stage's crash not to get hurt.

"Howdy Malvo. I would ask how you're doing, but

I doubt you're doin' too well right about now." The gang leader snickers as his eyes twinkled.

"I'll be doin' better than you as soon as the tables turn," Malvo said in such a calm voice you would think he and the outlaws were friends. "Why didn't you stay working as a cowboy? I don't believe that outlaw life will fit you too well."

"Keep on talkin', and you're gonna be riding across the back of your horse, dead, Tanner."

"I know that's not true, or you would have killed Chito-Ochi as soon as you saw him. I know Sheriff Egan wants us alive. You know as well as I do, he doesn't have any evidence of us committing a crime. He hopes to lock us away until we're forgotten. Like I said, it's a long way to San Antonio from here. We'll see who dies along the way."

As soon as they robbed all the passengers, they mounted up and stormed off just as quickly as they arrived. A dust cloud followed them like dogs chasing rabbits. They had Malvo, Chito-Ochi, and our horses. As soon as they were dots on the horizon, I found the courage to climb down from the tree to rummage through the remains of the stagecoach, looking for something of value left behind, but these thieves were through, and they left little that I could use as a weapon.

I watched as the passengers limp back the way they came. Some had broken arms and cuts on their faces. Although they all looked worn and battered, they were all alive. Still, I didn't want them to see me either. I had no intention of returning to El Paso when my friends were kidnapped before my very eyes. I didn't know what, but I had to do something, but something told me not to trust anyone.

I began following them across the hot, dry desert for lack of anything else to do. I walked for the rest of the day until I saw the sun sitting squat on the earth's rim. I stood with my head down against the glare with my hat pulled low over my eyes. I passed my dry tongue over cracked lips. I checked my Colt Walker revolver for the hundredth time, which made me walk to one side. I wondered if I would ever get used to the weight. I weighed almost five pounds loaded.

A prism of colors shot across the sky just before the night claimed the day and rushed it away as stars rolled out like a carpet and the moon rose on the opposite side of the world.

The wind whispered in the grass. Owls hooted in the darkness as coyotes howled at the moon. Dry earth and gravel crunched under my feet. Occasionally, I would squat and run my fingers over the tracks like I've seen my friends do. I had to keep calm and think, what would Malvo or even Chito-Ochi do if they were in my situation? Unfortunately, I couldn't even fathom their thoughts and continued like a pilgrim following the North Star.

Unruly hair hung from the shadow of my white Stetson, a wide-brimmed hat, thick and glistening from the heat. Sweat stained my shirt front and back as it stuck to my skin, but there was no turning back. At least the tracks of numerous horses were easy to follow, plus I knew exactly where they were headed. I wondered what happened to the passengers as they walked back to El Paso. In this heat, I don't doubt they had a hard time. Luckily, I was already broken in and trained by Malve and Chito-Ochi and knew how to survive in an apparently unsurvivable country.

alone and afraid

I continued to walk into the night by the light of a pumpkin moon. Chito-Ochi had told me these vast areas were populated by savage aboriginal tribes; in this part of Texas, the Comanche and Apache were the most feared Indians. I wondered if I made myself little; I might sneak by without being detected. I did as my new Indian friend taught me and tried to walk between the shadows even while traveling at night.

My boots crunched gravel underfoot. The sound echoed in the night. I felt like I was making as much racket as an elephant. Was it my imagination? Still, I did as I was taught and walked on, waiting for the first light to appear on the eastern horizon.

When I looked back, I believed I could see the glow of yellow lamps in distant El Paso, but when I looked east, there was nothing but darkness. Like Malvo had taught me, I traveled twenty yards off the main trail to avoid encountering unseen trouble. Every time I thought I heard something, I dropped to the ground and made myself as small as possible. Still, I worried about snakes.

I remember Malvo telling me, "If you dance with the devil, the devil doesn't change. The devil changes you."

Now, I wondered what he meant. Would he and the Choctaw Indian survive, or would I arrive too late? Even when I got to San Antonio, how would I find them? If they were locked up in jail like the Crowder brothers said, how could a fourteen-year-old break them out? I still had more questions than I had answers, but I knew they would do the same for me as they had in the past. Come hell or high water, I planned to do the best I could.

Benji heard something in the night, and his eyes flicked from one shadow to another, looking for signs of an ambush. He had no idea who could be out there. He knew that Texas was full of men of reckless blood who had found their homes in ruins back east after the war and rode to Texas where they wouldn't be detained, arrested, or maybe hanged. The Union army was taking notes and writing down the names of those they believed committed war crimes. Some were fabricated to suit their needs for revenge, and others were truly evil men.

Texas was part of the South and the Confederate States of America. It seceded from the Union in 1861 and joined the Confederacy. Over seventy thousand Texans served during the war. Even though the state governor, Sam Houston, steadfastly led Texas to be loyal to the Union, in the end, it sided up with the

South and seceded. Most of Texas didn't own slaves but were against the federal government interfering with the rights of Americans. In the end, the governor from 1859 to 1861 helped force the holding of a public referendum on succession on February 23rd and eventually opposed joining the South.

As the South built an explicitly White society of pro-slavery and an antidemocratic nation-state, its slogan was that *all men weren't created equal*. In 1860, there were one hundred eighty-two thousand enslaved people in Texas brought by White families from the southern United States. At the beginning of the war, it claimed its solidarity with its sister, slave-holding states.

The war had changed many men. Farmers, ranchers, fathers, and brothers became mortal enemies, tearing families apart. As the conflict raged on and the violence grew deeper, many died for the promises of restitution after it accused northern politicians and abolitionists of committing a variety of outrages against Texas. Yet, the state didn't experience many significant battles, although the Union made several attempts to capture the Trans-Mississippi regions along with Louisiana. It eventually became a blockade-running haven.

Suddenly, my hearing became hyperacute. I felt like I could hear the rodents running across the dry leaves that had fallen from the trees. I was filled with conflicting feelings, unleashing a cataclysmic storm inside my brain. Suddenly, I felt like crying. I forced back the feeling and bit my lip until it bled. There was no room for babies in the middle of the Texan desert. I had to buck up to the challenge and take it like a man, or I would not only fail to save my best friends but would also die in the process.

I heard a creek gurgling nearby, so I made a beeline for the sound, dropped to my knees, and had a long drink. I didn't know the country, so I had no idea when I would get another chance to acquire the refreshment to carry on. Luckily, I brought the goat waterskin from the stagecoach. It was one of the few items of value left after the robbery. At least I wouldn't die of thirst. I scooped water into my cupped hands and rubbed it on my face while washing the dust away. Beads ran down my chest and back as my mind cleared as I cooled off.

First, I heard hammering hooves in the distance. They sounded like they were getting nearer with every minute that passed. I didn't know if they were Indian ponies or shooed horses. I heard a gunshot not more than a stone's throw away, making me dive for cover into a briar patch. Then, someone made sounds like men do when they are badly wounded and are afraid of dying. For a fourteen-year-old boy, I had heard those sounds far more times than I'd ever expected.

They were the same groans my family made as I held on to the cold, wet rope at the bottom of the water well while hiding from our Comanche assailants. From then on, my life changed, and I had heard men die on several more occasions. Even though I was a young boy, sometimes I felt like an old man.

As I hid, I heard more hooves beating the hard ground. When I caught sight of the Apache Indians, they looked like hungry wolves but maintained their distance before skulking away into the brush. These weren't your successful type of Indians. They were poor and dirty, wore ragged clothing, and rode skinny ponies like the defeated men they were. Lucky for me, they didn't discover I was there. As soon as the sound of their hooves disappeared, I got up and started walking east again, just off the main trail.

Inwardly, I let out a long breath of relief and then snickered to myself. "Act like a man and don't cry, huh?" I chuckled despite my fear. "Why, I still have to learn what a man is."

Late that night, I sat exhausted from the tension as I stared at the small dung chip fire. I made it deep in an arroyo so nobody would see the light. For a moment, my mind drifted to my family and what once was. Although I missed them, I knew that fretting over what had happened did me no good. It just made me feel lonelier. So, I focused on my objective. I didn't know what I would do when I found Malvo and Chito-Ochi, but I somehow thought I had to try. It was time I returned the favor.

On my way eastbound across Texas, I saw a herd of longhorns as I passed them at night. Malvo said they were distant descendants of abandoned herds left by the Spanish a hundred years earlier. I turned for higher ground in case they stampeded, but they didn't even turn my way. I was so small I wasn't even perceived as a threat to the animals.

As I walked, I tried to reject fear, but as a fourteen-year-old boy, it was hard. He knew that now I couldn't act like a frightened little kid because I was on my own and nearly lost. Still, I continued to follow the tracks. Sometimes, they were confused on the well-traveled road. I passed cold fires I could only assume belonged to Indians. One of the cold camps held the remains of a dog on a spit. The coals were still warm, so I knew they wouldn't be far away. If they were the same Indians, I could only guess.

Finally, I saw the first hint of red in the eastern sky. Soon, I saw the orange disk peek over the world's rim. Surprisingly, I saw a silhouette not a mile ahead of me. His shadow grew long as the fiery disk rose into the sky. Luckily for me, I didn't run into him at night. I had no idea who it was, but I decided to take a chance since he was alone. I fingered my heavy Colt Walker revolver to give me confidence. I doubted he would find me a threat and shoot me dead, but this far west, you just never knew, so I wasn't going to take any chances. The metallic sound of the hammer echoed in the silence. Still, the man before me didn't stop or look back.

I hurried my pace, but the single man and mule continued their trajectory eastbound. It was clear that they were minding their own business. I wondered if my interruption would be unwelcome, but I knew I would have to take a chance. I felt too vulnerable all alone in such a vast land.

Finally, I was two steps behind him. I knew he could hear me if he weren't deaf, but still, he didn't turn his head. Gray, scraggly hair peeked out from under a weather-beaten hat with a floppy brim. The aparejo on the horse's back was loaded down with battered mining equipment and burlap sacks. The mule looked to be as old as the man.

"Ain't you scared being out here on your lonesome?" the miner asked without looking back. "You didn't think I saw you, did ya? When you live out here long enough, you learn to notice anything that moves. I take it you saw that Apache war party. They were looking to steal horses to eat. It looked like they were starving. Lucky for me, they didn't fancy my aging mule. They knew she would be like old leather and hard to chew."

"Honestly, I'm scared stiff most of the time." I raced to catch up. "The land is so grand it makes me feel as small as an ant."

The old miner slapped his knee and said, "Good for you, boy. Spoken like an honest man. Be honorable above all else. You've got grit; I'll give you that. The truth is if you don't have a wagonload of courage, you'll never make it in this country. Not with this heat and nothing in between one town to the next, not to mention the wild animals and Indians." The miner chuckled humorously, shaking curtains of long gray hair and beard. "My name is Junior Adams. And what's your name, young fella? And what are ya doin' out here all on your own?"

"I'm Benji Willow. I'm going to San Antonio if I don't get lost."

"Well, that's a coincidence. So am I. You *do* know how far it is, don't you? It's five hundred miles from here as the eagle flies." He held the flat of his hand to his eyes and stared into the distance, but he still didn't look my way. "You're alone, you say?"

"Yes, sir," I said as Junior tried to manage a smile and finally looked at me with twinkling, foggy eyes.

"And now come you're all alone? You can't be ten years old."

"It's a long story. We didn't have two pennies to rub together when I was younger, but we got by just fine. I can remember being in a happy, loving family once upon a time. I never went hungry for a day. That is until the Comanche came and killed my folks and brother. He was my twin, and it was our birthday. I'm fourteen."

Even though I tried to hold his gaze, I looked away after a few seconds, but his stare didn't falter. I didn't know if I should confide in the strange miner or tell him a lie. Then again, I wasn't much at telling tall tales. I figured I'd take a chance and see how things worked out and tell the truth. Malvo always said to lie to a man you just met started you off on the wrong foot. My ma always said it was a sin. That's one of the things we learned from the Bible when she would read it by candlelight at night.

Junior stopped so suddenly that his mule bumped into his back. "You're an orphan, then, are ya? Well, you're welcome to travel with me. Mind ya, all I've got to eat are beans and the odd rabbit, prairie dog, or squirrel we might scare up. But I can assure you that you won't starve. I don't see much of any provisions on ya. You don't look like you planned your trip too well."

"The truth is, I was riding with my two friends. We

were working as guards for the Butterfield Stagecoach Company, and the stage got robbed."

"Your friends got killed, I take it. You might want to tell me the which of why you're out here all alone."

"No, sir, they were tied up and taken to the sheriff in San Antonio by four thieves. Malve Tanner and my Choctaw Indian friend are bounty hunters, and I ride with them. They found me after the Comanche killed my folks and burned our home. If it weren't for them, I wouldn't be here. The outlaws said a bounty was on their heads from some sheriff who had a grudge against them. Malvo shot his brother, but that's what bounty hunters do. They hunt their outlaws and take them in for justice unless they resist. From what I've seen, Malvo would rather take them alive than have to shoot them. The sheriff's brother didn't give him a choice."

"Now, don't tell me. Let me figure it out. Do you intend to walk to San Antonio and break your friends out of jail? For such a young lad, you sure do have a set of stones on ya. It sounds like you've got a full plate, though. Making the long five-hundred-fifty-mile trek is a major feat. Especially for a young fella like yourself."

I swiveled my gaze at my new friend. Or at least I hoped he was. He was right about me not being prepared. Junior cocked a brow and looked at me like I was crazy. But then he shook his head and grinned.

Junior Adams lit the stub of a cheroot, inhaling deeply as he observed the situation and tried to figure out the right thing to do. "Well, I can't just leave you out here, can I? I'm heading for San Antonio anyway, so you might as well walk with me. Just be careful of my mule old, Nelly. She tends to bite folks she doesn't know."

When Junior found me, he saw my face was pale white and glistening in fear. Now, I felt my brow and mouth relax, knowing that I wouldn't have to try to get to San Antonio alone. When he wasn't looking, I glanced up and mouthed, "Thank you, God." But I made sure Junior didn't see me. I still didn't know if he was a religious man or not.

"In a couple of days, we'll be in Pecos City, where we can purchase supplies. It'll be best if I do the talkin'. I've been traveling this route for neigh on twenty years, so the townsfolk know who I am and leave me alone. To them, I'm just a poor, old, unsuccessful miner in ragged clothes. Why, sometimes they don't even notice I'm there."

"How many towns are there between here and San Antonio?"

"This stretch of road is called the Lower Emigrant Road. It's an economically important trade route here and all the way to San Antonio and beyond. Mail, freight, and passengers make their way overland across the Edwards Plateau. It's the Tans-Pecos region of West Texas."

"Do a lot of people travel back and forth? I see more signs than my friend and the four outlaws. Chito-Ochi taught me how to read different tracks. I'm a quick learner—especially for my age."

"John Coffee Hays attempted to find the route to El Paso in 1848 along with a squad of Texas Rangers. They spent three months on their quest, but they failed. Hays only made it as far as Presidio. It wasn't until 1849 that Lt. William Whiting and Lt. William Smith finally found this pass suitable for a new route. They constructed Fort Inge, Fort Clark, Fort Lancaster, Fort Stockton, Fort Davis, Fort Quitman, and Fort Bliss to secure the travelers and the mail and keep the stages running. It's two hundred and ten miles to Pecos north of Fort Stockton and Fort Davis."

We walked through the day telling each other stories of our lives. Although my life was short, there was more packed into fourteen years than I had realized. I felt like I was talking all day, but when the afternoon came, I felt better having gotten all that had happened off my chest—and to a total stranger, no less. Junior was easygoing, a good listener, and a patient man. He seemed honestly interested in everything I said.

He, in turn, told me stories of his adventure mining across the state. He said there was vast wealth under Texan soil. All you had to do was locate it. He had been at it for twenty years, and according to him, he only dug up enough to survive. He mined along the Llano River in West Texas near the Rio Grande. Men came from the Civil War, and because they lacked a better choice, many took their chances mining for gold.

He also told me that in 1865, the Comanche were present but not as violent as in their large, unified presence in the past. Still, the situation was complex and evolving. That very year, the Treaty of Little Arkansas aimed to establish a reservation in the Texas Panhandle, but the Comanche didn't settle peacefully. War parties dotted the countryside, wreaking revenge on the whites for stealing their land.

During the day, we used a burlap sack to collect dung chips for the fire. As the sun neared the world's end, fireflies flashed all around us, and crickets began to chirp. That night, we slept in a gully, making it impossible for someone to stumble upon us. Old Junior was good at going unperceived, but he did so in plain sight. He looked so poor that few men would waste their time stopping and trying to rob an unsuccessful miner.

Junior didn't even carry a pistol. The only firearm I saw was an old, twelve-gauge shotgun. The stock was worn and unpolished, yet the gun was well cared for. An oily sheen covered the large double barrels.

The next morning, I woke up early. As soon as I opened my eyes, I saw the stars still twinkling overhead. For a moment, I panicked, expecting to see the miner long gone, but there he was, breathing deeply as he dreamed. His feet and hands moved in unison until I cleared my throat and brought him out of his deep sleep.

For a moment, Junior stared at me, all baggy-eyed and confused. It was early in the morning, and he had yet to get his bearings anew. He shook his white-haired head to clear the cobwebs, then grinned, showing his crooked teeth.

I frowned. "Would it be dangerous tryin' to break my friends out of jail?"

"Dangerous? Everything in Texas is dangerous, son. Lots of brilliant ideas are risky." Junior smiled. "If we travel like two poor miners, nobody will pay us much attention, though. We'll have to do something about your fancy store-bought clothes. To go unnoticed, you've gotta look the part. Most folks around here are looking for something to steal, but if you show nothing of value, most of the time they hardly acknowledge your presence."

My gun suddenly felt unbearably heavy, and it was too big to hide on my small body. "Where do I put it?" I held my pa's Colt Walker.

"You picked yourself a power-packed pistol. No matter where you hit a man with that, you'll take them down. Skinny out of those fancy duds. I have an extra pair of overalls you can use until we find something better. And hide that cannon you're wearing around your waist. Stash it on Nelly somewhere deep in the mining tools. Then it'll just be another piece of metal. Leave it where you can get to it if you need it. The local Indians and outlaws alike would give their teeth for a gun like that."

When I changed clothing, my pants legs dragged a foot behind me, and I had to hold my loaned britches up with one hand. Lucky for me, the old miner wasn't a big man, but I still swam in the oversized britches.

"Shaw," Junior Adams said, slapping his hand to his forehead. "I plumb forgot you were so young and small. Roll your pants legs up and tie this rope around your waist. Well, don't just stand there like half-struck noon; we best get a move on."

After walking for a few hours, Junior said, "Lookee there; fresh horse droppings are on the trail. That means your friends are still going in the same direction."

"Maybe they're closer than we think."

"Out here, it's best to take your time. Moving too fast may cost you your life. It won't be the lack of water that bothers us. I know every waterhole from El Paso to San Antonio. It's the dust that drives some men crazy. Especially on these windier days."

Benji wasn't so worried about the weather but nervous about the Indians. All around them they saw signs from pony tracks, abandoned cookfires, and carcasses from animals they hunted and ate in bloody steaks.

three
captives

After riding for the rest of the day, they finally stopped about an hour before sunset. On their way, they collected dung chips from the road to use for their nightly fire. The outlaws knew exactly who Malve Tanner and Chito-Ochi were, so they left nothing to chance. Both men had their hands tied to their saddle horns and a rope bound to each foot that ran under the belly of their horses. If they fell off, they would probably get trampled to death. The two Civil War friends exchanged glances.

They assumed that Beji had climbed down from the great oak tree when the other passengers turned around and headed back to El Paso. They believe he would be safe until they returned if they somehow escaped and made it back alive. Little did they know how determined the young boy was or how attached he had become to his only friends. Unbeknownst to them, he stole through the night while they rested for beans and a good rest. The five hundred miles that separated them were slowly slipping away.

During the day, they rode hard but stopped an hour before sunset and didn't leave until they finished breakfast two hours after first light. The Crowders did their job but didn't break their necks doing it. It was apparent they were of a lazy nature.

Malvo was confident with such a long journey; the Crowder brothers were bound to slip up sometime, and he didn't believe they had long to wait. He knew Sheriff Egan was furious and desperate. If he chose the brothers, nobody else would take the job. Even with his hand tied, they knew their time would come. Neither man had made it through the Civil War without having unusual cunning. At some point, their capturers would make a mistake, and they would be waiting, and when the time came, they would strike.

"Don'tcha think you're out of your league, Boyd? How about you, Darrel? I'm sure that Henry and Chuchu feel the same. How in the world did you get that name anyway?" Malvo fingered his empty sleeve.

"He's called Chuchu because he's like a train," Henry replied with a scalding chuckle. "Slow and stupid."

"You'll watch your mouth if you know what's good for you, Henry. Just because you're the oldest doesn't mean that you're the strongest. I can whop you with one hand tied behind my back. They call me Chuchu because when I hit you, it'll come with the power of a train."

They crossed the badlands where rocky outcrops

formed into mysterious shapes and shadows, creating dark places for a man to hide. It held a dark, desolate beauty with pink bands and black rock.

"All the muscles in the world don't make you a smart man. And why is it that Sheriff Egan has such a grudge against you two?" Henry asked. "He promised us a five-hundred-dollar reward each to bring you both alive. I don't know why he didn't just have us shoot ya. It would have saved a lot of work. Then we wouldn't have to take you all the way to San Antonio. I find it a complete waste of time."

"He hates us because we killed his outlaw brother." Chito-Ochi smiled. "Malvo shot him, and I scalped him for trying to kill us in an ambush."

"And why did his brother wanna kill ya then?"

"Because we meant to take him in for the five-hundred-dollar bounty on his head. He was wanted for robbery, murder in the first degree, and war crimes. The sheriff's brother fought for the South and the sheriff for the North. Somehow, William Egan felt responsible for how things worked out. We took the paper and chased him down for the wicked man he was, even if he was on our side in the war. His actions were despicable. The sheriff thinks he can lock us up on some trumped-up charge and keep us in his jail until he can figure out how to kill us and go Scott free. If you get caught, he can always blame you boys. Who is going to believe a Crowder? There ain't been an honest man in your family for decades."

"I can't say that it makes me feel bad turning in Rebel scum like you two. We won the war, remember? Your side lost, and to the winners goes the spoils."

"Don't forget, I'm a patient man, Henry. After we kill you four, then I aim to take care of Sheriff Egan, too. And it's not because he's a Yankee. The war's over, and he should know better. I'm not one to keep a grudge, but he was a captain in the Northern army and murdered his share of Southern captives. That or starved them to death so they couldn't say it was murder later. He just can't deal with his brother being no good."

That night, they chained Malvo and the Indian's ankles to another oak tree. They weren't taking any chances. They gave them just enough rice and beans to keep them alive and healthy until they could collect their bounties. Silvery lights fell through the trees like rain, leaving tiny dots on the ground and leaves rustling overhead. Somewhere in the distance, a wolf howled at the pumpkin-colored moon. Chito-Ochi's eyes shone like dark chips of polished obsidian.

"It looks like rice and beans again," Malvo groaned.

"I don't mind," Chito-Ochi said as he spooned food into his mouth like he was starving. "I've had worse. At least we don't have to cook ourselves."

After dinner, the Crowders sat around the camp-fire, passing around a bottle of store-bought whiskey. Cinders came alive, swirling into the sky to burn out and disappear. The flames cast shadows on the trees and boulders surrounding them, making the edges of darkness come alive. Soon, all four brothers were nodding off from too much to drink.

"They don't look like they're going to post guards," Malvo whispered. "They didn't learn much in the war, did they? At least they could have put the fire out. They believe because there are four of 'em and they're heavily armed, the Comanche and Apache will leave them alone. I'll take the first watch until midnight; then wake you up to spot me."

"At least everybody in this campsite is not stupid. I just hope we get away before they get caught out by some Indians who think their guns are worth the risk. Those weapons are ten times more valuable to Comanche than they are to White men. They have *our* guns too. We're going to have to get those back."

Before the end of the war, they had all been ready to fight, prepared to die. Some of the soldiers, both North and South, preferred to end their lives on the battlefields rather than return home to what they had heard and read about. The Union army burned homes and raised ranches to the ground across the South. The war was long over, but still, the hate-filled many men's hearts on both sides.

Malvo's face darkened as he spoke. In an instant, his eyes grew black and dangerous. "After we turn the tables on the Crowders, we'll have to visit Sheriff Egan. He's supposed to uphold the law and not break it. We've gotta deal with these idiots, then get to San Antonio before the sheriff gets wise."

"You are taking a lot for granted. We have to get away first. They may not be the brightest brothers, but they all know how to shoot."

Cinders rose on thermal currents, vanishing above

the trees. Chuchu Crowder snored like a train. All of them were oblivious to the potential danger of recklessly sleeping in Indian territory. Malvo sat in the shadows of the tree to which he was chained. All that was visible was the whites of his eyes as he traced the dark for movement. He focused his hearing beyond the crackle and pop of the campfire. He had the feeling that they weren't alone. Maybe it was because of the fire.

He looked down at the chains binding his ankle and tested their strength. They appeared to be prison shackles and unbreakable, which meant that they would need the key the elder Crowder had. He watched Chito-Ochi lay sleeping beside him like he didn't have a care in the world. He was like that during the war, too. When he turned off his mind, he went to his peaceful place until he awoke to a new situation.

Malvo's mind was buzzing at a hundred miles an hour, searching for some minor mistake or lapse of security by the gang. They would have to deal with them and then ensure the mail pouches with silver were returned to their actual owners. He assumed there would be a sizable bounty for the stolen cash. But his Choctaw friend was right. First, they had to get away.

The following day, they rode with the sun in their faces as they continued to travel east. It was only a few hours after sunrise when they saw the first signs. Malvo and Chito-Ochi exchanged looks and then looked back at the ground. They saw the tracks of at least ten unshod Indian ponies. Considering where they were, they could be Apache or Comanche.

It didn't matter what tribe they were. Either one

would attack and was probably following them already, especially when they saw that two of the six White men were prisoners and couldn't defend themselves. They would think they were easy targets, especially after seeing how recklessly they traveled.

The brothers talked about what they would do with their new silver windfall. They not only had the money from the stage, but they would also have another payday when they delivered the two bounty hunters they held as prisoners. It didn't matter to them if they were innocent or not. All they cared about was the bounty money.

Boyd's mouth bulged, a tobacco wad accentuating the creases in his ruddy face surrounded by unruly black hair. He was a perfect example of the many inexorable men in Texas. He and his brothers would cut a man's throat for a dollar.

Malvo's rugged, square-jawed face looked as though it was chiseled from granite. He wasn't only powerful, he was deadly. His eyes glowed orange like branding irons in a fire. He and the Indian knew it wouldn't be long before something happened. They waited to see what their capturers would do before formulating their plan. If they were Comanche, they would come hard—maybe giving them a chance to get the upper hand.

He knew the Comanche were superb horsemen as they rode fast but with apparent effortless grace, trailed by a cloud of dust. When the war party caught sight of the Crowder brothers and their prisoners, they whooped and shouted as they neared. When the hostiles drew closer, they rode in circles around the outlaw's camp. Their images became hard to see from the dust kicked up from the horses' hooves.

They believed the White men were frightened, so they whooped and yelled even more. All the while, they stayed out of pistol range. Even with a rifle, they would be hard to hit as they raced by, blurring their images. Chito-Oche saw that none of them smiled.

"Don't shoot!" Malvo warned the Crowders as they drew their weapons. "You can't hit anything at this range anyway. That's what they want you to do: waste your bullets. Then they'll come at you when your pistols are empty."

"Shut up, fool. How many of them are there, Darel?

"I count near-on a dozen, or maybe as many as fifteen."

"There are ten," Chito-Ochi said dryly. "Didn't your father teach you to count?"

"Shut up before I scalp you, Injun."

"You won't be able to hold off that many warriors without our guns, too. The four of you will never win against ten armed Comanche. Unlock our chains, or you're going to lose your scalps." Chito-Ochi drew his thumb across his neck to make his point. "I don't want to die at the hands of those warrior braves any more than you do."

"Hell, no!" Henry replied with a voice full of steel. It was clear he wouldn't be moved. "You're wrong, just like all you Southern trash. I wish the war had gone on for another year, and we could have wiped your gray coats out once and for all. It was a mistake to settle the war, and I'll always hate General Ulysses S. Grant for allowing General Robert E. Lee to surrender April 9th. 1865 was a sad day in my book. Come on, boys, show 'em what we've got."

"Those trash aren't people: they're no more than prairie maggots," Chuchu swore before firing until his pistols were spent and his hammers fell on empty chambers.

A cacophony of gunfire roared as barrel flashes and smoke followed chunks of lead out of four hands full of guns. But as they were warned, not a single Comanche warrior fell.

"I thought you boys could shoot straighter than that. Why, you didn't even wing a single Indian. Like I warned you, you'll never make it on your own. You won't be spending that money if you're shot all to hell and dead."

Aboriginal people hunted the Great Western Plains for thousands of years. The original inhabitants witnessed the recession of the glaciers when the land began to warm. They accelerated the demise of the saber-toothed tiger, the great mastodon, and the hippo. They hunted the same land when it was densely forested. Now it was a sea of grass and desert. Through all these changes, the Native American Indians continued to live as nomadic hunters on these vast stretches of land.

The nineteenth-century Indians were colorful, mystical, and warlike. The antiquity of their rituals and the intricate organization of their many tribes compared to none. They were a hunting society built around the horse, even though the four-legged animals weren't present until the Spanish introduced them three hundred years earlier.

One of the Comanche veered off while the others continued to circle, running flat out. He drove his horse, whipping it into a frenzy. His grace as a rider was second to none as he raced toward the White men. He let his reins trail as he took aim and fired a worn Winchester. The rifle barked in his fists.

Duffy was surprised when his body jerked; he was shot, and before he knew it, he found himself staring up at the sky. He blinked as he struggled to catch his breath. Blood poured from the jagged hole in his chest.

"Duffy's hit, Henry!" Boyd cried like he was the one who was shot. Tears welled in his eyes as he looked in shock at his brother. A dark pool of blood formed under his dying body as he dropped to his knees at his brother's side. All it took was one look to see he wouldn't survive.

"You're running out of time, boys!" Malvo cried as the din of war continued. "Now you're ten to three, and your chances for survival are slipping away. Unlock our shackles, and we'll show you how it's done. If not, all of us are going to die just like your brother."

Henry frowned and shook his head in denial, but then he turned his gaze back to the circling Comanche, and his eyes spread wide in shock. Still, he didn't budge.

When the bullet hit Boyd's head, it snapped back, and his body followed. His boots dug into the dirt and toppled him over, spread-eagled on the ground. He was dead before he hit the dirt.

The elder Crowder's mouth was so dry his teeth stuck to his lips as his heart roared in his chest and hammered between his ears. Sweaty palms clutched at his rifle, and rivulets of sweat ran down his back despite the cold. He had forgotten that the men fighting by his side were his enemies. The dread of being scalped consumed his thoughts.

Malvo felt the anger rise hot on his face, but he forced himself to calm down. Now wasn't the time to make rash decisions. He talked softer, but there was still an edge to his voice. "Don't you dare move a muscle, Henry. You don't wanna end up like your brothers, dead and bleeding out. Now give me that key, or we'll all die right here."

Henry's eyes returned to the screaming Comanche and back to Malvo. Then he glanced at his dead and dying brothers. He knew bounty hunters by reputation and had been warned by Sheriff Eagon, too. But now he saw he was backed into a corner he couldn't get out of alone, so he pulled the pigging string from around his neck, jerked it off, and gave Malvo the key.

"You turn on me, and I'll shoot you dead," Henry threatened, but his voice had lost its thunder. He knew when he didn't have a card to play.

Malvo quickly pulled his Sharps rifle from its scabbard, threw it to his shoulder, and fired. The first shot hit the nearest warrior, throwing him into the air. He fell to the ground motionless. The second and third shots came from Chito-Ochi's rifle. Both animals dropped, buckling their knees and throwing their riders like wounded birds. They were left in a daze when they hit the hard dirt as Malvo took a bead on his next target.

A knot tightened Malvo's mouth. Still, the smile remained, but now it didn't reach his eyes and had lost its meaning. He looked at Henry like he was a dead tree, utterly free of emotion. Then he turned and fired again. The projectile roared out of the barrel and closed the distance between the gun and the target as the bullet shattered bone and ripped into his heart.

He opened the fifty-two-caliber, inserted another round, and levered it into the chamber, then slipped his finger into the trigger guard and fired again. All the while, Malvo listened to his thoughts flashing through his mind at lightning speed. Every movement was planned and intentional.

"They're gonna overrun us, Henry!" Chuchu screamed. "You tricked us, Tanner. Maybe we are all gonna die, but I'm gonna be the one who kills you."

Tanner rolled across the ground as his pistols came up, one behind the other, squeezing both triggers simultaneously. The recoil made the barrels jerk. Both bullets hammed Chuchu's back like he was hit with a sledgehammer. He blinked like he couldn't believe he was shot. He was so dumb he thought he was indestructible. His body went limp as he fell to the ground like a sack of potatoes.

Chito-Oche didn't wait and waded into the remaining Crowder, Henry, clubbing his face with his hammer-like fists. He backed him up onto a pile of rocks and hit him with a roundhouse haymaker. His eyes rolled back onto his head, and he slumped to the ground. When the Choctaw Indian nudged him with his toe, he moaned.

Henry managed to crawl to his hands and knees, look up at Malvo, and then returned their attention to the warring Comanche.

"What's he doin' flappin' his hand all around like that?" Henry groaned.

"He's making hand signals," Chito-Ochi said.

"Tell them I come in peace."

"You tell them. I see nothing peaceful about you, Crowders."

Henry remained silent from then on, and nobody asked any more questions. He already knew the answers. Still, the Comanche waited. They appeared to refuse defeat even though they had lost five warriors. They saw the other side of the coin and believed they had nearly wiped the White men out.

"It's funny how the tables can turn against you in the blink of an eye. But then again, I knew you'd screw up, Crowder. You were never as smart as you thought you were."

four
the aftermath

"What are we gonna do with Henry?" Malvo asked. "We'll be travelin' with a dead weight, and we'll have to keep an eye on him all the time. I guess we could take him to Pecos with the money. The sheriff there can lock him up until the El Paso law comes and fetches him to hang. That is if those Comanche leave us alone."

"How about we kill him and bury him with his brothers? Or leave them where they lay and let the vultures pick their bones." Chito-Ochi replied as he stared deep into the outlaw's eyes. To Henry, they looked like tombstones. "Remember, he would rather kill us than take us back alive. He said so himself. It was only the bounty money that kept him from finishing us off. What do you think we should do, Henry? Should we do to *you* what you wanted to do to *us*?"

They saw fear in Crowder's widespread eyes. His face begged for mercy, but neither bounty hunter felt pity for the outlaw. Only five Comanche warriors were left, and they stayed just outside Malvo's rifle range. It looked like they had learned a lesson. Usually, Indian war parties gave up after losing a man or two, but these were desperate times for the Native Americans. Still, the bounty hunters didn't believe they would continue to charge. Their losses were too significant, as were theirs.

An arrow whistled through the air before Malvo could get off another shot with his Sharps. It seemed to come out of nowhere, and they hadn't seen any Indians with bows in their hands. Not with rifles and pistols going off like popcorn in a skillet. Still, it snuck through their defenses like a rattlesnake with its deadly strike.

They heard it fluttering like a bird before they saw it, but then it was too late. The arrow protruded from Henry's neck as his bloody hands struggled to dislodge the projectile. The Crowder elder dropped to his knees and then pitched forward. He lay on his belly, face down, as his stiffening fingers clawed at the hard dirt and gravel. His legs began jerking in spasms as the life drained from his body.

"I reckon that's the end of that. Do you have any more questions?"

They watched as the Comanche warriors turned and rode off. Minutes later, they vanished over a distant ridge. Everything around them fell silent. The smell of gunpowder hung strong in the air. Crows cawed from the bare limbs of trees overhead, and the smell of blood drew the scavengers.

"Quick now, let's get the money, guns, and horses and skedaddle out of here," Chito-Ochi huffed. "I think we have worn out our welcome. There's an expert bowman out there, and we don't know where he is."

Tanner went over to his mare and tightened the cinch. He had to do everything with one hand, but he was more efficient than most men without missing limbs. It was obvious that he deliberately ignored the loss. He shrugged it off like it was a mosquito bite. It didn't make him less deadly. If anything, it made him more dangerous.

"I'd say now's the time to cut and run before some of those Comanche's friends decide to return and take revenge. How long do you think it'll take to bury the bodies? We can put all four in one hole to save time. I hate to leave even an outlaw for the vultures."

"It's too dangerous to take the time to bury these fools," the Choctaw Indian spat. "Remember, there's still five Comanche warriors out there looking for a fight. Just because we saw them ride off doesn't mean they've given up. And then there's the Indian with the bow. We don't know if he's left or not."

They grabbed the mail pouches with the money, their guns, and those of the Crowders. Then, they rounded up all their saddles and went through their saddlebags. They found documents identifying Henry and Boyd. They believed that with the little paper-work they had, the horses, and a few belongings, they had enough to claim a bounty on their heads if there was one. They knew there would already be a reward for the bullion stolen from the stagecoach. Money was always the most important, especially to the banks.

They mounted up and led the extra horses on riatas as they rode for the nearest town and the local law. They wanted to put some miles between themselves and the battle. They knew the Indians would be back later to reclaim their dead and give them proper Indian burials. They never left the courageous behind. There was no honor in being eaten by scavengers. They would be back to ushering their brothers into the Indian spirit world.

A dozen buzzards circled overhead. With each turn, they came lower and closer to their next meal. The vultures meant that everyone within a couple of miles would know that there was something dead just over the horizon. Men and animals alike would be drawn to the scene. Soon, the coyotes would come in packs. By morning, there would be little left of the Crowders.

Malvo and Chito-Ochi rode slowly and easily, ensuring they didn't ride into an ambush. It would be just like the Comanche acting like they were leaving, then lying and waiting to finish the job. They had already killed four of the six and might believe they had the upper hand. Then again, they saw how Malvo and Chito-Ochi used their guns. If they stood to lose more men, they may veer off and wait for them to leave. And leave was precisely what they intended to do.

After a while, Chito-Oche watched the black specks in the distance with the flat of his hand over his eyes. At first, he was suspicious. Dust devils crossed their intended paths as the black images wavered in the heat of the Texan sun. They gradually grew as they came nearer. Finally, the specks turned into moving figures, then into a mule, a man, and a boy.

"Well, I'll be danged if that doesn't look like Benji Willow. It seems he's found a new friend, too. I wonder what in the world he is doing following us. Don't he know it's dangerous out here?"

"What is he doing coming this way? He should have walked back to El Paso with the others. That young man never seems to stop amazing me. He is more like a Choctaw Indian than a White boy."

Malvo and Chito-Ochi dropped off their horses, tethered them to ground stakes, and made a fire. By the time the stranger, mule, and their young friend arrived, a hot kettle of coffee and some stale biscuits were awaiting them. The aroma of freshly perked java filled the air.

We lay around the fire that night in a yellow, flickering circle of light. Malvo eased onto his elbows with his back to his saddle and his hand behind his head as he stared into the fire. Chito-Ochi pulled his hat over his eyes and listened to the night birds chatter in the dark. Benji sat between the bounty hunters, grinning like a possum. Now that he could reflect on what had happened, he felt like he had experienced another miracle.

Overhead, the stars swung counterclockwise in their nightly course as the Big Bear turned and Earendel winked in the farthest distance. A comet cut a streak across the sky before burning out on its entry into the Earth's atmosphere. When the moon rose again, it appeared so close that I felt that I could reach out and touch it. Silver light shone on my sunburned face.

"So, whatcha got to say for yourself, young man? Why didn't you go back to El Paso and safety? What did you think you were gonna do? Save Chito-Ochi and me from the stagecoach robbers? You're a might small to have such big man's plans."

"I reckon I really didn't have a plan, but I knew I had to follow and try." Then I started questioning what I had done and hoped my friends wouldn't be mad. "Lucky for me, I ran into Junior here. He's been riding these trials for over twenty years."

"I'm a miner by trade, but as you can see, I ain't all that successful. I reckon that I'm fiddle-footed, is all."

"You're alive. Out here, that is the ultimate success." Chito-Ochi smiled. "Not many men can say they lived here for so long and tell the story from some-place other than a grave. In this country, a man survives by his wits and brains and not by bluffs like those boys who abducted us."

While the others seemed like they wanted to talk, I couldn't, no matter how hard I tried to stay awake. I was so tired from walking day and night and all the tension about not knowing what happened to my friends I was dead on my feet. My eyes became so heavy they drooped and then closed. Soon, I was snoring softly. My Choctaw friend scooped me up in his arms and laid me in my old bedroll, where I slept all night and late into the morning. My friends didn't have the heart to wake me after Junior told them my story. They could hardly believe how loyal I was.

I heard Malvo say somewhere in my dreams, "He's fourteen years old, goin' on twenty." I felt my lips curl despite my deep sleep.

At first, I had nightmares. I once again saw the battle scene and remembered how my heart sank until I saw that my friends weren't among the dead. Still, the scene was as frightening as anything I had ever seen. But after a while, my mind turned off, and I fell into a deep state of slumber and forgot about everything. My body didn't move for hours.

The dusk thickened into light when the first rays of the sun reflected in the sky. Late the following morning, Tanner raked the toe of his boot through the dirt, pushing it over the dying fire. "We should clean our campsite up with all those dead Indians back there. They'll notice the Crowders, too. It's best not to leave too many signs of our presence or where we're going. We can ride off the main trail for half a day. By then, we should know if we're being followed or not."

I pondered as I took a sip of coffee before I spoke. "I saw the Comanche and the dead outlaws who robbed the stage. At first, I feared for your lives. I've never seen such a terrible scene. Well, maybe, except for seeing my family murdered. Anyway, I sure am glad I found you two and that I didn't have to try to break you out of jail."

This surprised and enthused all three men. At first, my comment brought chuckles and snickers. Then they all laughed until they got a stitch, but I didn't see what was so funny.

"Why are ya laughing? I wasn't joking. I was gonna

break you out. I even told Junior what I planned to do, although I must admit I didn't quite know how I was gonna do it." I couldn't stop my smile from stretching from ear to ear.

After a good breakfast, I swung into my familiar saddle, pushed my fists into the small of my back, and arching away the stiffness from sleeping for too long on the hard ground. I was still worn out from walking for so long with little rest or sleep. At the same time, I was elated. Although I hadn't done anything to help rescue my friends, I knew they were both proud of me for trying, especially striking off on my own and walking all night.

That was the only reason I could catch up, along with the hours they lost in the battle against the Comanche war party. In the end, it paid off to walk nonstop, never letting up or giving up hope. I felt that in the last weeks and months, *hope* was the only thing that got me through the next day.

Suddenly, I realized how certain I was about my intentions. I never doubted that I would find them despite the situation. Looking back, everything pointed to an impossible mission in an improbable dream. But to me, it didn't seem like something I couldn't do, even if I didn't have a plan. I had confidence, and as Chito-Ochi said, I had a wagonload of courage. He had said it with heartfelt conviction, so I knew it was true. Hadn't he mentioned it, I would never have thought it was possible.

My father's Colt Walker hung heavily from my waist. I wondered when I would grow into the holster, and it would no longer feel so big in my hands. I knew I had a lot of growing up to do, and I saw more every day that I had little time to do it. Next time my friends were in a jam, I intended to be better prepared despite my young age. I wasn't feeling like a little boy anymore. Every day, I felt more and more like a man.

I always found that violent conflicts proceeded with near silence save the dying. It was just like that after the Comanche killed my family until I heard Malvo ride in to save me. Again, the conversation waned for the first few hours of the day. Nobody seemed to have much to say. Of course, I had a million questions like always, but I knew now wasn't the time.

"If you wanna break off from us, I'll understand, Junior. We're a target until we get rid of all this silver. I remember you said that it was best to travel like you were poor if you didn't want to draw attention. With all these horses, we're gonna be a target if we run across a gang of outlaws or some more hostile Indians. I won't think bad of you if you do decide to continue on your own, and I'm mighty grateful for you letting me ride with ya."

"Did Junior tell you that?" Chito-Ochi asked. "He's one smart cookie, then. But maybe he's fooling us all, and he's a millionaire from a gold vein he discovered in one of his mines. There have been dozens of fellas who have struck it rich in those hills. What's the biggest strike you've had?"

"Me, a millionaire? I don't even know what that would look like. Do you? Do I look like I've got more than twenty dollars? My mule ain't worth much more. If I had any money at all, I'd be riding a stage in comfort."

"I've read about rich folks living like hermits." Malvo grinned. "Mind you, I don't know exactly what I would do if I had so much money either. I doubt it would change my ways much. I only know how to do the one thing we've been doing since the beginning of the war. Money hasn't meant so much to me after all that. It's a necessity of life; it is what it is and not much more."

"To Indians, money means nothing. It is something that White men invented to create greed for what others owned. Wealth is in here." The Choctaw Indian poked his thumb on his chest. "Many people think that the land belongs to us when the truth is, we belong to the land. Any Native American knows that, but the White people think they own everything they can stake out and fence. When they're gone, the land reclaims itself, and the owner turns to dust. Mother Nature is the only constant out here, and she will ultimately be the only one who can survive."

"I've never thought about it like that," Junior said. "I'll have to keep that in mind when I return to my mines and return it will. I've been diggin' for gold for so long that I don't remember how to do anything else. In the end, I'll probably die in one of those holes I've dug."

"And, if you're so poor, why is it you've gotta go all the way to San Antonio to do, Junior? That's where all the big banks are. It seems like a long way to walk or ride for no reason." I blinked like a bird, waiting for his answer. Now that I thought about it, it did seem odd.

"Why, I do it every year. I suppose it's become like a pilgrimage. As far as banks, I've hardly stepped foot into more than two. I sell what little I find at the local merchants or the general stores. They all have scales. Like I said before, I'm fiddle-footed, I reckon. Now, I believe you boys won't be going all the way to San Antonio anyway since you have recovered the stolen money from the stage."

"We'll have to stay a few days in Pecos, but once we're done with the bank, sheriff, and whatnot, we'll head to San Antonio to see an old friend. Or maybe I should call him a foe. One of the city's sheriffs falsified a wanted poster with our names on it and sent the Crowders to kidnap us while they robbed the stage. That means that Sheriff Egan knew what they were up to. There's more to this than meets the eye, but he's already done enough to have a county judge lock him up. Sheriffs are voted in, so half the politicians will be with him and the other half not."

"Maybe he even provided them with information about so much silver being on the Butterfield Overland

Stage," Chito-Ochi said, rubbing his hairless chin. "That's normally not public information. We were hired especially to guard the money, but the Crowders wrecked the stage and caught us off guard. Maybe they weren't smart enough for such a clever plan. Maybe they had more help than we thought. I reckon they paid the price, though. Now it's time for Sheriff Eagan to fess up. All we've gotta do is get to him before he gets to us."

They walked their horses through the boiling hot day, occasionally standing in their stirrups to peer into the distance. As they rode, their heads swiveled from one side to the other, taking in everything around them. Benji kept an eye out for dust clouds. He had learned enough that they were usually accompanied by trouble. Heat wavered in the distance, making every-thing appear to move.

As usual, Chito-Ochi rode point, ensuring they didn't run into an ambush or highwaymen. There was little law in this part of the state. The Choctaw Indian slouched in the saddle, one leg hooked over the saddle horn as he waited for his friends. When they caught up, he swung his boot back into the stirrup. Now, they had to be extra careful. Especially with the Comanche knowing they were there. At least nobody should know about the money from the stage robbery, which was in the mail pounce over the horses' rumps. There were two hundred miles between El Paso and Pecos. Now, with so many valuables, it seemed like a long way.

My tongue slid over my cracked, dry lips. I pulled my hat lower, leaving my eyes in my brim's shade.

Junior chewed on the end of a dead cheroot. In the end, he chose to ride with us to the next town but didn't mention whether he would continue to San Antonio or not. I could see his point. Seven good horses and a fine selection of guns would tickle any Indians' fancy. At least they would be after the stolen money.

We reined our horses down the long grade as the sun was almost overhead, crowing the sky with its bright, white light. Shadowless riders rode toward the barren horizon as tumbleweeds rolled by. I pulled my bandana from my neck and dabbed my eyes. The sweat from my brow rolled down my face.

The Choctaw Indian vanished again for a few hours. When he returned, he said, pulling up to a stop, "I saw more horse tracks, but I don't think they were from the Comanche war party. I only saw two sets of hoofprints, both shod."

When the sun began to set on the rocky horizon, a breeze stirred. It whispered through the trees and bushes, giving relief after the glaring white heat of daylight. We spent another quiet night in dangerous country, but this time in a cold camp. We didn't want to risk getting the attention of the two riders, whoever they might be. Under the circumstances, it was better to ride with only men they knew and, when possible, go unperceived.

Of course, Junior was above suspicion. He had done the right thing and allowed me to travel with him, winning the hearts of my best friends. My spyglass inched over the expanse as the country yawned wide, but I saw nothing unusual. Still, I searched the horizon for signs of movement. I didn't want to get caught unawares again. As it was, I was lucky I didn't break my neck when I was thrown from the stagecoach.

"Tomorrow, we'll hit Pecos sometime before sundown if we don't run into any more trouble," Tanner said. "Once we get there, we can get rid of this money and relax for a while before continuing east."

As Malvo took the last watch, he saw the sliver of red in the blackness to the east and knew it would soon be daylight. Boots made muffled, scraping sounds as they moved over sand. Since we had a cold camp, we had to forgo our coffee and had stale biscuits. We slowed and picked our way through briars and brambles, always staying a distance off the main trail.

Pecos had a rich history in West Texas. Its location as a crossroads for cattle drives made it an important hub. It began as a cow camp near the Pecos River. The small town grew into a city as a livestock distribution and service center. It was the crossroads for overland transport for many years. Horsehead Crossing was where thirsty cattle stampeded to the river's steep banks after being driven from San Angelo, seventy-five miles away. Two years after the Civil War, it became the Goodnight-Loving Trail. Some of the drives were all the way from Fort Sumner to New Mexico and Colorado.

Just after the Civil War, Pecos was a rough-and-tumble frontier town known for its violence and its role as a cattle drive center. The city had a reputation for its lawlessness, where gunfights were common. It attracted reckless individuals in droves, and after the war, there were countless men with no hope who fed on what belonged to others. We knew we had to be more careful with every step toward town we took.

The area was also known for its ranches and farms. Underground aquifers enabled the production of crops like cotton, onions, and cantaloupes. Despite the violence, many men came there with their families to settle on free land. Its proximity to Fort Stockton and the convergence of the two main roads across Texas made it important. Its location made it a major hub for stagecoach lines, even though the flat, dry desert was as inhospitable as the men who populated it.

Dust danced in the light, falling through the trees and making yellow spots on the ground. I stretched my neck and gulped the hot desert air.

Behind us, we heard the faint, faraway rumble of a stagecoach. The creaking, churning wheels and jingling harnesses raced by in an explosion of wood, leather, and horseflesh. A dust cloud followed the stage like dogs chasing rabbits.

We cocked our ears to the sound that was still a whisper. As it became louder, we heard the familiar pitch to the clamor of the stage. We saw the driver throw his boot at the brake lever, and the coach jackknifed to a stop. The dust slowly began to settle. We suddenly found ourselves on the edge of town and in front of the waystation.

I pushed my hat back from my forehead, easing the hot grip of the headband—narrow hips, sun-darkened, thin-lined features beneath the brim of my faded Stetson.

No sooner did we guide our horses into town than

the suspicious marshal stared at us with his thumbs hooked on his gun belt. He stepped off the boardwalk and into the middle of the street. It was almost like he was challenging us.

At first, Malvo showed surprise, but then he relaxed into a grin. "How ya doin', Marshal? You're just the man we were looking for."

Chito-Ochi's hands were gripped over the other, leaning on the saddle horn as we patiently waited for the town's law to reply. However, he didn't budge and stood there waiting. His mouth was no more than a hard line.

"Stay put until I have a word with the marshal." Malvo stepped out of the saddle, letting his reins trail.

I could see the iron-willed anger in the tight line of the marshal's jaw. A brittle silence hung over the edge of town. For a town welcome, it wasn't much.

For some reason, the county marshal was tight-jawed and solemn. As soon as we locked eyes, he frowned. Behind him, I could see cowboys in leather chaps and large hats. Some lay sleeping in the shade of porches, and others were obviously drunk. After the quiet on the lonely trail, the town was busy with the hustle and bustle of a growing West Texas city. Horses, mules, and buckboard wagons raced up and down the street. To me, the town law looked hard-shelled and mean.

Malvo Tanner had the sort of face that needed the brim's shadows to soften his sharp, gaunt features and hard lines. If you didn't know him, you would think he was angry most of the time, and right then, he wasn't hiding his displeasure from our unwelcome reception.

Chito-Ochi gently flicked the rein against his horse's neck, easing him forward as his hand inched toward his gun. As an Indian, he didn't entirely trust lawmen, at least until they proved their worth.

"What are the likes of bounty hunters like you two riding with a little boy and a broken-down miner?" It was clear that the marshal didn't like strangers despite the fact the town was full of the same. "That's right, I remember who you are. We don't need any more gunfighters in town. I've got enough problems on my hands as it is."

"I didn't know we were so famous," Malvo replied. "Especially way over here in West Texas."

"Bad news travels fast. We might be off the beaten path, but we do have telegraph wires and newspapers, even if they are a month or two old. I've seen both of your faces on the front page."

"We're not here on a friendly visit. We caught the outlaws holding up the stage outside of El Paso and recovered the stolen silver to deliver to the bank. That and have you make us a check for the bounty money."

"And how am I supposed to know that you two weren't the ones who really robbed the stage?"

"Then, why would he ride into town to see the local law and give the money back to be returned to the Butterfield Overland Stage Company? That would be a foolish thing to do for outlaws, wouldn't it now?"

With a tobacco wad in the marshal's cheek, his lips

hardly moved when he talked. He slowly shifted his chew to the opposite jaw.

"Uh-huh, that's what they all say," he replied. "The name's Mashal Lem Boone, and I run this town. If you mind your manners, you might just stay out of trouble. I know who you are, Tanner, and the Choctaw Indian with you, but I still don't know what you're doing with this young fella. What are you doing mixed up with these two, Junior? I've never seen young boys ride with gunfighters."

"Gunfighters and bounty hunters were different things last I heard." Junior smiled, showing a mouthful of crooked teeth. "I found the boy on the trail a day's ride out of El Paso. He was following his friends to help them out of a jam."

"Now I've heard everything. Whatcha got to say for yourself, young man? Come on: cat got your tongue?"

I neck-reined my horse toward the hitching rail as Chito-Ochi urged the string of horses to follow. I urged my horse with a rowel to the mare's flanks.

Malvo's eyes—white caged in rigid, red lines. I could tell he was getting angry.

Suddenly, the marshal's eyes shifted: "Behind you, quick!" Boone dove for the porch floor as he pulled his gun.

Suddenly, bullets zipped through the air, cracking as they broke the sound barrier. Everybody on the street scattered like roaches when light spilled into a dark room. Chunks of lead slammed into walls, support posts, and even windows as glass flew everywhere like tiny knives. At the end of the short street stood two men with a brace of guns in their fists. Flame and smoke spewed out of their barrels.

Malvo felt his patience quickly fading as he fired twice in one smooth motion. The marshal was still attempting to take aim when the assailants dropped onto the street, motionless. Tanner hadn't flinched when the town law threw himself to the ground in fear for his life. A dirt cloud filled Boone's nostrils with dust as he looked up at the bounty hunter. Smoke squirreled from the barrel of his gun.

"Like they say: you never know a town until you've spent time in its jail." The marshal stood, removing his hat to dust off the dirt. "I'm gonna lock you boys up for your own safety. Now that you've killed two of the men from the Cowboys Gang, we'll all be safer sleeping in the jail. Luckily for us, I don't have any prisoners right now. Judge Roy Bean sends most outlaws to swing from a tree." The flesh on the back of the marshal's neck tingled from the scare. He had felt one of the bullets as it whizzed by his head. It nearly parted his hair. "That was too close."

"Don't just stand there like twelve o'clock half-struck," Malvo said, eyeing the sheriff as he looked up from the ground. "Get up, and let's get this gold and silver into your jail before one of these brash men finds out we have it and tries to take it from us. I have no idea why those two were gunnin' for us."

"They were after me," Boone replied. "In general, marshals don't have many friends in a town like Pecos."

I suddenly felt the tenseness in my breast, and my ears felt tingly, making every muscle instantly tighten.

Long strides took Malvo to the marshal's office entrance three doors down. His face: a bronzed, hard mask matured beyond his age. When he removed his broadband hat, thick brown hair hung close to his skull. It glistened with oily preparation.

I paused to catch my breath and wiped the sweat from my face with a grimy hand. I hadn't had a bath in days. Suddenly, I noticed the bad smell and wrinkled my nose. Then again, maybe it was the odor of fear.

Marshal Lem Boone shook his head wearily, clearing his throat before speaking. "I reckon I owe you an apology, Malvo. An inch closer, one of those bullets would have taken my head off." He stared wide-eyed and swallowed repeatedly. The shadows of the horses' legs were like black elongated sticks.

"Chito-Ochi, you stay here with Benji and Junior and make sure nobody steals the loot. The marshal and I will go out and see exactly who it is we shot."

Thirty strides took them to the bodies in the street. Malvo pushed the dead man, who was face down, over with the toe of his boot. His sightless face had dirt stuck to one side. A bullet hole punctured his ribcage. The other was shot right between the eyes. There was no question that they were dead.

"Occasionally, the lion has to show the jackals who he is," Malvo said, then spat a stream of tobacco juice on the dead outlaw's face.

A whirlwind stood like smoke as the dust swirled around, racing down the street. Lem stood, wiped his mouth, and stared at Tanner, wondering what he was going to do. He was clearly the man in charge.

The bake-oven air didn't rebate with the setting sun but continued into the night.

"We'd better get back to the jailhouse before somebody finds out we're in town.

"Everybody knows you're in town already, Mr. Tanner."

"Call me Malvo, all my friends do, Leim."

When they returned to the marshal's office, they found shotgun barrels in their faces.

"Put your guns down, boys. We're the good guys."

Once inside, Lem's pencil ceased to scratch the parchment for a moment as he stopped and thought, then began to write again. "Who should I make the check out to, Malvo? Things went to blazes in a handbasket there for a minute there. Hadn't you two been here, I might have been shot and killed."

Late into the night, Malvo eyed the strange old man over the flicker of yellow kerosene lamplight. He knew Junior was hiding something, but he couldn't figure out what it was. If he weren't, he would have ridden off as soon as he heard they had the outlaw's loot from a robbed stage. Like Benji had asked, why was he going all the way from El Paso to San Antonio if he was as poor as he said?

The earth floated off in a long curve to the world's end. On the edge of town, under the moonlight, clamored with yapping coyotes amid cries of owls. A wolf lingered like a marionette from the heavens, his long mouth jabbering and saliva dripping from his tongue. Thunder muttered somewhere in the distance as heat wavered on the horizon.

Tethered dogs howled at the edge of Pecos as they bared their teeth and snapped at one another. Night birds chattered with the wind as vultures rose from the ground, their bony wings flapping and whooping like children's puppets on a string. Just to be safe, he knew that he had to figure out who Junior was before they let him ride with them to San Antonio.

rich man - poor man

For the first time in my life that night, I slept in a jail cell. It was one place I thought I would never see the inside of, but here I was. Still, the straw mattress was softer than the hard ground I had been sleeping on for the last few days, and I couldn't think of a place where I felt safer. Who in their right mind would attack a marshal's office and jail—especially with Malvo Tanner and Chito-Ochi inside? As far as the brash sheriff was concerned, my opinion of him remained to be seen. I noticed he wasn't very friendly, at least not at first. Then again, I reckon a marshal couldn't be nice to everybody and keep the law.

Beside me in the next bunk, Junior snored like a bear. When my eyes opened, and I took a deep breath, I discovered we *both* smelled bad. For the first few moments, I stared at a water stain on the ceiling, wondering how many outlaws did the same before me and what their thoughts were. Some of them were probably on their way to the gallows. If jail walls and bars could speak, I could only imagine what secrets they might tell. Wherever you die, it's still the same distance to Heaven or Hell, even if you're in jail.

The marshal had a bunk at the end of the five cages. It had a mirror on the wall with a wash pan under it on a small table. A rope rug lay beside the only bunk. Malvo and Chito-Ochi shared another. Surprisingly, I was the first to awaken, so I had time to study their faces. I grabbed my boots and Colt Walker revolver and tiptoed to the kitchen. Malvo taught me always to keep my sidearm handy. You never knew what the future would bring, and if your gun wasn't accessible, it could cost you your life.

I flicked the end of a match with my thumbnail, sparking it to life with a puff of smoke and the smell of sulfur. Then I lit the ready-made kindling, and in seconds, the fire started. Soon, crackling flames flickered under the gallon coffee kettle. As I rummaged around, I found bacon and eggs and made breakfast for everyone. I hoped the marshal didn't mind, but I planned to pay him back for the dozen eggs and pound of bacon if he did. As soon as the meal began to sizzle, I noticed Malvo and Chito-Ochi's noses wiggle. Then, a harrumph came from Marshal Boones's cell.

"Is that breakfast I smell?" Lem asked. "Maybe you're smarter than a regular kid your age. In these parts, the way to a man's friendship is often through his stomach." He chuckled to himself as he pulled his boots on and stood, slipping his suspenders over his shoulders and snapping them in place with his thumbs.

"Is sunny side up all right with you, fellas?" Like big yellow eyes, egg yolks stared at me from the grease-sputtering skillet.

"Fry up plenty of bacon. We can repay the marshal as soon as we cash our bounty check for the stolen money." Malvo stood, pulled his gun belt from a wall peg, and slipped it on with one hand. He slammed his loaded 1851 Navy Colts into their holsters, one at a time. Then he slipped his Winchester rifle into the crook of his arm and turned.

In less than two minutes, I had all three men sitting at the only table in the room. Once I laid their tin pie pans before them, I sat and dug in. Steam rose from the food. I didn't know how hungry I was until that first spoonful of steaming eggs touched my tongue. I scoffed them down like a hungry tiger, using stale bread to sop up the yolk. Not a word was said for a moment as everyone devoured their meal. The only sounds were knives and forks scraping tin pie pans. Soon, I poured coffee all around as brown bubbles popped from the kettle's spout.

"That boy scampers around just like a racehorse. If Malvo and Chito-Ochi get tired of having you around, you can come back here, and I'll give you a job sweeping up and making *me* breakfast every day. I'll even give you a deputy's badge if that makes you happy."

"Maybe." I shrugged. I was being polite. Now that I'd found them again, there was no way I was leaving my friends. "I'll keep that in mind if my partners get tired of my company."

"Oh no, you don't, Marshal. Benji is part of my team now, and nobody is gonna take him from us." Malvo gave me a heartfelt grin that reached his eyes.

I drew in a sudden, deep breath as my eyes spread with delight. I always thought they felt the same about me, but my thoughts being confirmed was great.

"He does make some fine bacon and eggs." The Choctaw said as he stuffed the last bit of yolk-soaked bread into his mouth. "Maybe we can try something else tomorrow. I hate cooking."

"Then why do you?" Malvo asked.

"Because, if I didn't, I would have to eat your cooking," the Indian said, shaking curtains of black hair as he chuckled.

I pressed my lips into a tight smile, and my heart rate flew off the charts. I pushed a wisp of hair out of my eyes and gave my friends a hopeful smile.

They could all see the thankful excitement in my eyes. Malvo's mouth curled into a grin. For me, there was a brief instant when everything froze, like in a picture. That was when I realized how lucky I was to have two such friends. They almost felt like the family I had recently lost.

Malvo arched his brow and asked Junior, "So, are you going to tell us the truth or not?"

"Whatcha mean, Malvo—the truth about what?"

"Don't try to talk around it. Why did you continue to ride with us, knowing we were a target, and this story about you going to San Antonio for fun? I'm fiddle-footed myself, but nobody rides this God-forsaken land for nothing. Five hundred fifty miles is a long way for a man your age, or any man for that matter. Especially with the Apache and the Comanche, not to mention the outlaws."

Junior steepled his fingers as he pondered deep in thought. I gave him a questioning look. Honestly, I was surprised by Malvo's question as much as I imagined Adams was. "What's he talking about, Junior? Is there something going on that I don't know about? Whatcha mean?"

"You might as well come clean, Friend. Indians can always tell when White men lie, even if it *is* most of the time. Friends don't hide things from each other."

Junior bunched his lips as he weighed the situation. Sure, he knew he had a secret, but it would be dangerous if it became public knowledge. He weighed what he had seen and heard what these two bounty hunters had done. He felt bad fessing up because now Benji would know that he told a fib even if he thought it was the best course of action for everyone.

Maybe I've been selfish thinkin' about myself too much, Junior thought.

The miner's breath was trapped somewhere in his body, and he felt like he couldn't breathe from the pressure. He knew no matter what he said, his secret was doomed to be known. He was suddenly drenched with sweat, and his hair matted to his head. He couldn't help but feel guilty.

"Be decisive. Right or wrong, go for it and stick to your plan. The trail is full of flat squirrels, Junior." I even surprised myself when I said it. All three men looked at me with shock and awe.

"I confess. I didn't tell the whole truth. I ain't poor anymore like I told you, Benji. I'm sorry for telling you a lie. I've been diggin' out here for twenty years, livin' as poor as a church mouse. But I've been off guard ever since I did strike it rich. I know what I found, but honestly, I don't feel right yet and don't know if I ever will. What does a rich fella do, anyway?"

"Whatcha mean, Junior? You mean you ain't poor anymore? You look poor to me. I don't think I quite understand what you're saying."

"You certainly are a suspicious character, Mr. Tanner. I'm on my way to San Antonio to put my gold in the bank. After twenty years, I finally struck it rich, but ever since, I've been terrified that somebody would find out and steal it from me. Sometimes, I wish I'd never found that vein of gold. It was as thick and long as a horse's leg." Junior couldn't help but give a meek smile. "I reckon I'm the richest man in the room by a hundred times or so. All I've gotta do now is get it to a bank somewhere safe. The small banks in West Texas get robbed as often as women change their underwear. I haven't dared to ask for advice because I figured they'd rob me for sayin'. Gold changes men quickly. I've seen it myself over the years but never thought it would be me to strike it rich. RICH? Whey it's just a four-letter word."

I couldn't help but blush red from what he said. At my age, I had never thought about women's bloomers. Embarrassment flushed my neck and cheeks as I stared at my boot's toes and tried to dig a hole in the floor. At the same time, I was shocked that Junior told me such a big fib.

"You've gotta understand, Benji. I didn't do it on purpose. I was even worried about your safety when you joined up with me, especially after you told me about the stagecoach robbery. That was why I made you wear my old clothes. It is true that poor men rarely are bothered by the likes of outlaws or highwaymen. Even the Indians only have a peek and are usually on their way as long as I don't steal their game."

"So, how much do you think your gold is worth?" Marshal Booneasked, his voice full of suspicion.

"I don't have the exact rate, but I reckon more than fifty thousand dollars or about five hundred pounds. That's why I've got Nelly. She's the biggest mule I could find. Mind you now, I don't know what that would look like in silver and gold coins."

The room went so silent that you could hear a mouse fart. Everybody struggled to imagine so much money. They doubted that Andrew Johnson, the president of the United States had that kind of cash.

Malvo whistled a long note. "Compared to the stage robbery, what the Crowders stole is peanuts. Now, I know why you didn't tell anybody. I wouldn't be offering a lot of information on the matter if I were you, either. So, I reckon you did right. Maybe, in the end, it will all work out for the bunch of us, especially if you hire Chito-Ochi, Benji, and me to guard you and your gold. We're all going in the same direction, after all."

I slapped a fly away with my hat while I looked at

my new friend in a different light. "I didn't know that folks could have so much money. I'm not even sure what being rich represents or how you would go about it."

Chito-Ochi squatted on the floor, dangling his hands in front of him with his elbows on his knees. He looked at Junior and then at me and smiled. "Indians don't think much of money, or even gold for that matter."

That evening, as we sat on the marshal's porch trying to figure out what to do, as ladies of the night lounged on the saloon balconies. Their faces were painted with indigo and Almagro, and they looked gaudy in their cheap fabric and skimpy clothing. I couldn't help but wonder what their bloomers looked like. The word seemed to have gotten stuck in my head.

As Malvo said, I'm fourteen and going on twenty. An involuntary smile graced my face.

Would they be in bright colors, too? I looked to my sides to make sure my friend didn't imagine what I was thinking. Without knowing it, I reckoned I was growing into a man. My curiosity was going wild. When I inhaled patchouli oil, it lingered heavily in the air. The women hid part of their faces behind their handheld fans, and their eyes blinked with lurid coyness.

"How much do you two wanna charge me to guard the gold until we reach the San Antonio National Bank?" Junior asked, embarrassed that he had to lie to his new friend, which was me. I instantly saw it was natural for him not to trust a couple of bounty hunters. Especially if he didn't know them. But I saw it in his eyes that he felt lousy about telling me a fib.

Many men on the street wore long mustaches and wide-brimmed hats with high crowns. In West Texas, they all wore big ten-gallon hats to keep the sun off their heads. Spurs jingled on cowboys' boots as they walked up and down the street in groups of five or more. The younger ones appeared almost to be shy. Twelve-year-old buckaroos walked with their older friends, trying to look grown up when they had yet to grow hair on their faces.

I drained my glass and nearly choked. I had to excuse myself and head for the alley before I embarrassed myself. I dropped into the shadows and hurled. It burned as it forced its way out, but that knot in my stomach disappeared. I was suddenly wobbly on my feet, but I bucked up, pulled myself together, and went back into the saloon.

The sheriff harrumphed and curled a sly grin. "And what about me?"

"Whatcha mean, what about you? You already have a job, don't ya?" Malvo replied.

"Well, whaddaya say, Junior?" the marshal asked. "I can ask the mayor for a few weeks off, and I know you can always use an extra hand, especially if he has a badge. That tin star will get you out of situations you might not wanna be in."

The idea of my latest friend having so much gold, which represented more money than I ever thought existed, fueled my resolve. It made blood race through my body, and my nerves began to fray, making me even more edgy.

"Maybe," the miner replied, shrugging his shoulders.

I could see it in his eyes. He had to weigh the marshal's honesty. He had known him for a few years, but usually, he was unfriendly. But then again, he had that kind of job. "And what are you gonna do about the job you have? Do you think it's worth risking losing your employment?"

Boone's heart suddenly began to thump in his throat. He knew there would be a big payday if he were hired. The marshal was an honest man, or at least as honest as a layman could be in West Texas. He didn't break the rules, although sometimes he bent them to his needs.

The old miner bunched his lips and shrugged. "It all depends on what Malvo and Chito-Ochi say about it. And don't forget Benji Willow. He has a say in this, too. I'd never have met any of you if it weren't for him. I'll be hiring them for the time being. Then again, we might want all the help we can get."

"I reckon we can use the help. How about it, Malvo? I'm sure Junior is gonna be generous. I think that the four of us can do this."

As soon as Malvo said yes, my blood sped into overdrive, and I let out a loud sigh of relief.

"Attaway!" Chito-Ochi said as he slapped his knee. "And here I thought we wouldn't be paid to go to San Antonio. Now, it's a win-win situation. We can take care of that no-good Sheriff William Egan and get good wages while we're at it. If it's that much money, it will cost you, Junior, but Malvo and I will see that you and your gold get there in one piece."

Junior looked relieved as he let out a breath; he felt like he'd been holding it for hours. "Boy-oh-boy, am I glad to have gotten that off my chest. I've never had to lie in the past. But I still think we ought to keep all this a secret if we can. We've already made a lot of noise with the stage money and the shootout as soon as we arrived. Everybody in town knows we're here."

"One has nothing to do with the other," Marshal Boone replied. "There are shootouts here nearly every day. What happens now will be forgotten later. Hell, most of the cowboys are here today and gone tomorrow and replaced with more new blood. Pecos is like a machine that takes their hard-earned money and sends it on its way. At least those young fellas have a good time while they're here unless they shoot each other."

"It doesn't matter," Malvo said. "He's right. We've already made too much noise. Keeping totally quiet ain't an option anymore. I think the best course of action is to act like everybody knows what we're up to, then we won't make any mistakes. Still, we need a plan before we make another step toward San Antonio."

Chito-Ochi nodded in tight-lipped affirmation. He knew they could use the extra guns with such an amount of gold, but he also knew that the yellow mineral made White men do things they wouldn't normally do, and it all came down to one of man's curses. Greed is what did funny things to most people. Some of them can control it, and others cannot.

Greed was something the bounty hunters knew all about.

As Tanner headed for the door, grinning, he winked his approval. "Come on, partners, we've got a check for cash. We ain't rich, but for us, it's enough."

Junior swallowed appreciatively, nodding his head. When his eyes grew wide, it was impossible for him to stifle a smile. He wondered if his new friends could hear the bass drum hammering in his chest. His amused smile grew bigger. His look was lit with elation—and vindication.

"You White men are crazier than a dog humpin' a pig." The Indian looked at his White friend with curious concern. I could see him relax the hard lines of his jaw, his face rugged and leathery until he looked at me, which brought a smile to his face. It softened his feathers and made him look kind.

The Pecos City Savings and Loan was just down the street in the relatively small town. It was the biggest and only painted building on the block. Two men sat on either side of the door as they nodded off and on. They had sawed-off scatter guns in their laps. With their attitude, they didn't look like they would be alert enough to ward off a serious robbery. Still, it was the only bank in town.

When the clerk counted nine hundred dollars, my eyes lit up like a Christmas tree. I nearly dropped to the floor when Malvo gave me my share. Three hundred dollars was a lot of money for a fourteen-year-old just after the war.

"You don't owe me any money, Malvo. I didn't do anything to help."

"You did much more than most men would have done. You followed us with an unfailing conviction. A man can't put a price on that. Loyalty and honor are what make or break friendships. You did your job with flying colors, young man. So, who's gonna come up with a plan?" Malvo asked as he locked eyes with each of us and raised an eyebrow over his one eye.

war wagon

"Maybe if we go by stagecoach, we might have a better chance of getting there in one piece," Marshal Boone said. "If we're armed well enough, we might ward off bandits or Indians. We can make sure no innocent parties are involved by purchasing all the seats. Then all we have to do is hire a stagecoach driver or two to make the trip."

"Won't that mean that somebody else will know what we have in the wagon?" I rubbed my nose and sneezed. "I thought we were supposed to try to keep this a secret if we can." I held my breath as my nose tickled and I sneezed again.

"We tried that once, and it didn't work out at all," Malvo replied, frowning. "The Crowders managed to stop the stage, and they ain't all that smart. Unless Sheriff Egan from San Antonio came up with the idea of digging a hidden trench along the coach's route, I'd tend to believe the latter. I doubt he'd stop at anything if he'd go far enough to make up fake wanted posters with the intention of making false arrests."

"But maybe there's a better way," Junior said. He had a voice in the matter since he had all his gold to lose and was paying the way.

"And what's that?" I didn't know if my two bits were wanted, but since I got paid so well for the last job, I didn't want to be left out of this one. "Maybe it'll be better if we sell the extra horses and ride off the trail like you taught me, Malvo."

"It's always worked out that way in the past," Chito-Ochi said. "Why should we change things now? As far as I know, nobody knows about Junior's gold."

"That's our first mistake: believing that nobody knows what we're up to," Malvo pondered. "That's what got us into trouble on the last job. Had one of us ridden out a few miles on point, the robbery wouldn't have succeeded."

"I won't discount the stage, but maybe we can do it another way. What if we build something like a war wagon? I saw the odd one during the conflict, not by us Southerners but by the Union. They used them to transport weapons and ammunition. If we borrow or rent one of the Butterfield Stagecoach Company's rigs and reinforce it so it'll withstand any attack they throw at us, we might make it there in one piece *and* with Junior's gold."

I had to remind myself to breathe again. I wondered if the others could hear my heart patter in my chest. This looked like it was going to turn into our biggest adventure yet.

"If we build something like that, it'll be hard to keep this a secret at all. Especially in such a small town as Pecos." Malvo fell silent for a moment. He mindlessly drummed his fingers against the wooden handle of his walnut pistol grip. "Everybody is gonna want to know what we're up to before we're done. What does a sack of gold look like, Junior? You said the vein was big, but how much space does it take to bust up into nuggets? Are all those burlap bags full of gold?"

"Yeah. I wanna see it too. I've never seen real gold besides coins, and those came from Malvo when we were paid for doin' jobs." I had to force myself from hopping up and down.

"That's why you insisted on carrying your mule's aparejo into the jail and close to you over there in the corner, ain't it." The marshal's eyes were drawn to the burlap sacks and mining tools. "Is it in there?"

"One of the sacks is my food, but the rest is gold." Junior nodded as all our eyes went to the supposed mining equipment. "Some of the nuggets weigh as much as a thousand grams. That's more than two pounds: a kilo. I reckon altogether it weighs about five hundred pounds, give or take fifty pounds."

"Why don't we leave it where it is for now," Malvo said. "We don't want to get ourselves all worked up over something that ain't ours. Here in jail should be safer than storing it in the bank. Then, by this afternoon, the whole town would know."

"We can lock it in one of the cells for the time being. I've got the only key." Lem couldn't take his eyes off the burlap sacks, then looked back at Junior. He knew he couldn't beg, so he stared at him with pleading eyes.

"How about this?" Malvo asked. "For now, we'll lock it in a cell. Then, later tonight, when things quiet down, Junior can give us a peek at what we're gonna risk our lives for. I need a few cups of coffee and something sweet to eat right now. Where's the best place for some apple pie or a piece of chocolate cake, Lem? When I'm in a town, I like to appease my sweet tooth. I suppose I can call ya by your first name now that we're friends." Malvo smiled, showing a corncob of straight teeth, and his only eye twinkled like a little kid's. "How about a dessert, Benji? I always say there's always time for something sweet, whether it's morning, noon, or night."

Marshal Boone beamed and could only hope he would stand up to the test. When they had to pull on the two outlaws, Malvo shot them both before he could even clear leather, and he only had one hand.

"There aren't any real restaurants here in Pecos, but most bars serve food. The businesses don't want their cowboy customers to wander off until they fleeced them to their last penny. First, they head for the general store and haberdashery to buy some new duds; then, they make a beeline to the saloons to get drunk. And when they've gained enough courage, they approach the waiting ladies of the night. Not long after, they're all penniless and broke. Mind ya now, the odd buckaroo deposits his money in the bank, but they only make twenty-five bucks a month, so if he keeps a few coins, it doesn't amount to much."

A long, oblong pine table stretched across the small saloon, and benches lined each side for when the cow herders sat down in groups to drink and eat. A squat potbellied stove and a door sat at the end of the building. A sign over it said, NO ENTRY KITCHEN. All the windows were open as the morning draft festooned the curtains. The cross breeze gave them some reprieve from the heat. Shiny brass objects were scattered across the room. Tobacco spit stained their sides. Wood plank floors were bare and scuffed. Bullet holes from times past peppered the ceiling and were patched with adobe mud.

"This is my regular stop," Lem said, leaning his forearms on the bar like he owned the place. "The bigger joints are full of painted cats and fallen angels with a few soiled doves sprinkled in." He cocked his hips and hung on the bar like it was something he often did, "Whiskey, coffee, and five glasses, Pedro. And dish us up whatever dessert you have to go around. We'll sit at my usual table by the window. Try not to send any cowboys over to eat near us. We want to have a private meeting." Lem dropped a few small coins on the bar top.

A sign hung above the bar, in red letters against a white background, reading MOONLIGHT BAR & TAVERN. Outside, TAVERN was all that was painted on the barren wooden wall. It, too, was fire-engine red.

A man with wiry red hair, a goatee, and a mustache stood over six feet tall as he pushed his way through the double doors, mumbling to himself. They noisily whooshed close behind him. In his formal dress, stiff collar, and frock coat, he looked down his nose at the marshal and his new friends. Stopping for an instant, he quickly evaluated the strangers and instantly decided he didn't like them. He wore lifelike painted wooden false teeth that clacked as he spoke.

"I see you've got some new friends. I don't know if I like the company you're keeping lately, Marshal. I usually don't see you with any friends. The way you men carry those guns says you're gunfighters. What do you have to say for yourselves, gentlemen?"

I watched him stare at my best friends with one eye asquint, but he didn't even seem to notice I was there. I knew I wasn't going to like him much.

"This is the town mayor, Lard Lumbard," the marshal said. The words hissed between his lips. "Lucky for me, I ain't elected, Mayor, and I can do what I want, not what you think is right or wrong. The mayor claims that America's future lay in the development and civilization of the West."

Mayor Lumbard proffered his hand like a good politician, but his was damp and cold.

"Ah hah. You finally see now, don't you?"

The smug look froze on the marshal's face. Malvo's keen eye saw his apparent distaste for the politician.

"The thing is, I don't see any civilization around here, Mayor. Lookee over there at Herman the Undertaker. Two more men dead for nothing."

One of the bodies was already loaded in the wheelbarrow when Herman Cross grabbed the handles and pushed him toward the coffin maker. Both establishments were busy day and night. A sign above the smell of sawed pine and the sound of hammering said, "Pecos Funeral Parlor." Freshly built wooden coffins leaned against the wall, some tall and some short.

The mayor stared at what he considered infamous bounty hunters like curious anatomical specimens from another world. From the look on his face, he seemed to enjoy and even invite heated arguments and discourse. Then again, they might disgust him, but they also scared him. He could instantly tell they were another breed apart, and he had better watch what he did and said. Some people didn't care if he was a mayor or not. He knew the marshal was one of those men.

"You will be sure to advise me if anything new pops up here in town, won't you, Lem? Everything affects how town politics work."

"Whatever you say, Lard. You want me to inform you whenever some cowboy shoots another, too?"

"I'll leave you to deal with the riffraff."

Mayor Lumbard's face turned red as he shook with rage, but he bit his tongue not to make a show. He would get even with Marshal Boone later. No low-life marshal was going to call him by his first name. The false friendly face disappeared for a second as he showed his true feelings. He obviously didn't like the marshal taking the same liberties as him. Although it was only for a second, it was long enough for Malvo and Chito-Ochi to catch. They immediately distrusted the politician.

"Remember what I said, Marshal. If there is anything new in town, I want to know about it forth-with." He growled, turned on his heels, and stormed out the swinging doors. His hammering boot heels disappeared into the distance as he stomped away.

Raised eyebrows, silently asked the marshal what was up with the mayor, but he brushed it off. "That arrogant fool is up for reelection next year. Most mayors in Pecos only serve one term. My job is permanent, so whatever he says goes in one ear and out the other." Pointing, he chuckled as he emptied his glass of whiskey in one go.

I was beginning to like the town marshal despite his initial attitude. Now I could see what a hard job he had with someone like Lumbard looking over his shoulder, hoping to catch him in a mistake or even worse. Still, he obviously had the grit to keep some semblance of peace in such a wild town.

When we finished eating, and it was time to leave, I could hardly wait. I had heard about Pecos but wanted to see around town for myself. I stepped onto the rectangle of sunlight carpeting the doorway and tiptoed to peek over the batwing doors.

"Don't be shy. Lead the way, Benji," Chito-Oche said, grinning like a possum. "I like being in the company of a man with a badge. It keeps the nosy White folks from poking fun or insulting Indians."

"If the cowboys are drunk enough, it won't matter. Sometimes, they even come looking for a badge to challenge. The same goes for the outlaws who ride through. Most of them were working on building their reputation. Then, they meet me and turn up dead. Still, I've gotta overlook most of the things they cowpokes do. Many of them are just young fellas, much like you,

Benji. They're the bread and butter for most of the town's citizens and their businesses, too. I'm here to keep them safe and happy. That goes for the cow herders, too."

When we walked down the streets of Pecos, I saw a wall of wooden storefronts. There were saloons, bathhouses, boarding houses, bars, taverns, hardware stores, haberdasheries, and brothels. A short ride provided every man's needs. Mixed in with the cowboys and Easterners seeking to strike it rich were a large share of immigrants from Europe.

They parked their overland wagons at the edge of town and away from the riffraff. Everybody knew how reckless cowboys could be. Sometimes, most of them spoke foreign languages and only had a translator or two to meet their needs for the stretch of land they had to cover before they reached the next fort or town.

Pecos was built with thousands of visiting cowhands in mind. At the other end of town was an oblong, thick-walled log building with several open stables and two large corrals at each end. One was for visitors, and the other for six-horse teams. On one side, they held the Butterfield Overland stagecoaches, spare wheels, barrels, and seats. Circling the way station, fifty yards out, was another five-foot-four wooden fence to protect the coach and animals and keep unwanted people out. In the old days, it was built to ward off hostile Indians who had their eyes on their valuable horses. They could make the station guard out, standing in the shadows of the doorway.

The sign perched on the top of a wooden post at

the crossroads said Main Street and River Street. The latter ran down to the Pecos River. Malvo's shirt stretched tight around the shoulders of the heavy-boned man. His buckskin-clad Indian friend was a few inches shorter and wore his hair in twin braids. Both had leathery, sunburned skin.

"Now that I'm full, I could use a bath and get a haircut. It's been months. I reckon we need a bath, don't we? We must smell like polecats after that ride across the desert." I noted that some of us smelled worse than others. Especially Junior, who I hadn't seen change his clothes or wash since we met him. My yellow hair hung down into my eyes. It was too short to hook behind my ears but too long not to cut.

The barber busied himself trimming Malvo's long locks and shaving his face, finally dipping his fingers into the grease bucket and twisting the tips of his mustache into sharp points. I waited in a stiff-backed chair. I knew I was next. Until then, I had never had anyone cut my hair but my dead mother, and that was only every three or four months. The idea of getting a proper haircut in a real barbershop was an experience I looked forward to.

"So, you're next, young man," the barber said.

He wore a knee-length, dirty apron and piles of brown hair lay all around the barber's chair. As soon as I sat, yellow tufts of hair began to float toward the floor, making it stand out from the rest. I had to stop myself from gasping when he brushed my face with shaving cream. I've never needed to shave, but I had the odd scraggly hair flowering on my upper lip and chin. The look on my face made my friends chuckle, but they bit their tongues. I was glad they didn't make fun of me. It would have made me feel less like a man than I already did.

Junior warmed up creakily, reluctantly saying, "I reckon I'm next." It was obvious that he didn't like the idea, but the fact was that he was the scruffiest-looking and smelled the worst of the four.

"We can't ride with a man that looks like a bum, no offense, Junior." I hoped I didn't hurt his feelings, but I didn't want to spend another night in a cell with my new friend if he didn't clean up and have a bath. His beard was so tangled it looked like animals lived there. "We don't have to act or look poor anymore. We'll be riding to San Antonio in style."

"It wasn't an act, Benji. I've been as poor as a church mouse all my life, so it comes naturally to me."

We walked from one end of Main Street to the other, Marshal Boone pointing out all the good places to go and the dangerous ones, too. Everywhere I looked, I saw men in worn riding boots with used guns on their hips. I didn't see a man in town unarmed.

Completely without warning, all the nerves in my body went dead, and I froze like I was injected with ice. One minute, the two cowboys were drinking together at a porch bar when an argument broke out. I watched as things heated up and became intense. I sucked in a bolstering breath and gobbled air, hoping that what I believed would happen wouldn't. When they pulled their guns, I saw it in slow motion. It appeared to happen frame by frame, like a series of pictures.

Iron cleared leather as thumbs drew back hammers. One cowboy's bullet shot low, which buried into the plank floor. The other .45-caliber slug hit his friend dead in the heart, exploding into a red stain racing across his chest. Gunsmoke hazed the air as the smell of cordite filled my senses while my ears rang from the blast.

The winner's sigh rattled, realizing what he'd just done while staring at his friend who was alive just seconds before. They had ridden across Texas together. He snapped a look over his shoulder, saw the badge flash in the lamplight, and stormed off the porch and down a nearby alley. The young boy's lank, greasy hair fell around large butterfly ears while his buddy bled out on the floor.

"Those dad-gummed fools. I knew they wouldn't let me have a meal," Marshal Boone spat as he ran to the door, pulling his revolvers.

"Is it like this every night?" I was still in shock that with a bit of whiskey, two friends would shoot each other over nothing.

A tooth-clenched curse followed the marshal as he ran for the alley.

"That's about as sorry as a two-dollar funeral. Young boys killing each other like that. They couldn't have been over fifteen years old. Pretty much like you, Benji. Then again, maybe it isn't all that odd." Malvo shot me a concerned look. "Life this far west don't give young men much time to grow up."

I nearly jumped out of my skin when I heard the bang. I guess deep inside, I knew it was coming. What else could the marshal do? Right then, I knew I didn't want to be a lawman in a town like Pecos, where the rule of thumb was daily gunfights. No wonder the funeral parlor was among the busiest businesses in town.

Now, when I walked down the street, I thought I saw churlish-looking men sucking their teeth and looking around with crazy eyes everywhere I looked. My old enemy, paranoia, sat perched on my shoulder as it whispered into my ear. A sweat broke out on my brown streaming into my eyes, making them sting.

At the end of the street, as the sun near the world's end, it shot a prism of colors across a dimming sky. Twinkling stars rolled out across the heavens before a thick, dark blue blanket of outer space. Our shadows stood at our backs like black elongated sticks. Torches were lit along the walls, their flames casting flickering shadows on the streets. With sunset, the party seemed to intensify as the cowboys began to drink in earnest.

The wide clearing with orange glowing windows illuminated the crossroads. They could see people with big Western hats sitting around tables inside. The yellow glow of kerosene lanterns reflected in the slightly steamed glass, spilling squares of light out and onto the boardwalk.

Another gunshot rang out from a heavy-caliber revolver. We all wrapped our hands around the butts of our belted pistols. I sniffed and drew a breath.

The escaping cowboy rode through the dust in a pandemonium of teeth and white eyes until Marshal Booneput a bullet in his back. He slumped over as his horse dropped down to a slow walk. The gunshot cowboy teetered from one side and then to the other before tumbling off. He wheezed through his teeth and died.

The dry dust soaked up the blood as soon as it touched the ground, and the last ray of light of the day shone in his dying face. I was in such shock that I walked outside and past the end of town. The look on my face told my friends not to follow. From there, I walked far enough away to see the glow over the city of lights when the day finally waned. Lightning bugs flashed before my eyes and into the distance as crickets began their choir.

I sat perched on the topmost rim of a hill like a mis-flown bird. Right then, I felt that I was growing up too fast. It was one thing to see grown men shoot and kill each other, but when boys my age died, I was shocked at the reality of my situation. Right then, I knew that despite my age, inexperience, and lack of maturity, I was already among the grownups, like it or not.

eight
the overhaul

When we arrived at the Butterfield Stagecoach Company barns and stables, we were surprised to gaze upon a nearly new coach. It appeared to be in perfect condition. Our eyes spread wide in surprise and grins stretched across their faces. Maybe this was going to be easier than we expected. I hoped this time I would get to ride inside.

"Whatcha lookin' at? Why, that rigs is almost new. You don't think I'm a fool, do ya, Marshal? The stage I'm givin' you is inside that shed over there. All ya gotta do is move those old, busted wagon wheels and the rotting harnesses and pry those old double doors open. I'll warn ya now: that's the first stage we bought in 1858. She's got lots of miles on her, but she was built to last. We had to retire her from the route a few years back. I don't know what shape she'll be in now. But you can have her if you can dig her out, free of charge. I could use the old shed for storage space. All you've gotta do is make her roadworthy again."

What were initially happy smiles all around suddenly turned to frowns, squinting eyes, and furrowed brows. The shed he was talking about looked like it was nearly ready to fall down, but sometimes appearances were deceiving.

"Why all the glum faces? You didn't expect me to give you one of my pride and joys, did ya?" Zeek laughed until he got a stitch. "You'll be doin' me a favor by getting' that old rig out of there. It'll be nice to see her back on the road again, too. Back in the day, I was a bullwhacker and not a stable keeper, and that old girl was my rig."

"I guess beggars can't be choosers." Malvo nodded. "Benji. Help me roll those busted wheels and broken barrels away to see what we're looking at. Those doors don't look like they've been opened for a decade, and the hinges appeared to be rusted into one piece."

"Come on, boys, don't just stand there like five o'clock, half-struck. Everybody's gotta get their hands dirty today. While you're at it, y'all keep thinkin' about your payday waitin' in San Antonio. That should motivate you. I know it does me."

"If we make it," the marshal replied dryly, obviously unconvinced, once he realized the work ahead. But what he stood to earn was equal to six months' pay, if not a year. It all depended on how generous Junior felt once they got to their destination, if they did, in fact, arrive.

"You would have to start moaning before you've even seen the rig, wouldn't ya, Marshal. This job has made you a grumpy man, Lem. I remember when you first came here, you were as friendly as me. It's that dad-gummed job you've got that's makin' you sour. Oh, yeah, I'm sure it would do the same to pretty much anybody. What, with you having to shoot those young fellas and all just because they can't hold their liquor without getting into a fight? What this town needs is an ordinance to check your guns before entering the town. It's a lot harder to kill somebody with your fists."

"That's foolishness. You want visitors to give *me* their guns while they play? I'd get shot for sure. I doubt a single cowboy would agree to something as absurd as that. What would you do if I told ya to check your guns in Malvo? I doubt you'd take it kindly. You're dreamin' of a perfect world in an imperfect town, old pard. Remember, we just came out of a war, making it even more impossible. I know I'm not gonna give anybody my gun."

It took all three men, including me, more than two hours to clear the debris from the weathered double doors. Unwanted and broken tools had been there for so long harnesses were fused together with rotten barrels and petrified hay. Nobody had tried to clean this part of the stables in years. We all wondered what was behind those doors. Was it a nightmare or another gold strike? Everybody hoped that Junior was still on his lucky streak.

"This looks like the original Butterfield Stage build-ing. See where the new bit of barn was added on?" Marshal Boone ran his hand across the rough, splitting wood. "I had just arrived when they added on the new bit. This was once the most prosperous business in town. Now, with the new steel rails crisscrossing the country, stagecoach travel will be limited and eventually disappear.

"If that's any sign of what's waitin' behind these doors, it'll be a toss of the coin whether it'll be of use or not." Chito-Ochi studied their work.

"Yeah, well, it's gonna have to do unless you can come up with a better idea. We might wanna keep an eye on that mayor. I think he's more suspicious than he leads on. I saw his questioning eyes when Boone asked for a month's leave to visit his dying mother in San Antonio." Malvo rested his chin in his hand as he studied the task at hand.

"Of course not, but we're not gonna let that fool know what we're doing," Chito-Oche growled. "That man is up to no good, like most politically minded men this far west. It wasn't the White folks that took our land. It was them from Washington that gave it to any man who wanted to make a claim, and they did it all from thousands of miles away where they were safe."

"If we don't move quickly, rumors will start to spread, and you know how gossip is," Lem added. "Nobody cares if it's the truth or not, especially in Pecos. The town is full of men of reckless blood."

"Bring me that long crowbar from over there in the corner, Benji. It's time to see what's in here," Chito-Ochi said. He grabbed the rusty crowbar and pried as hard as he could, grunting like a bear, but it only budged an inch. "Bring me that wheel axle, Malvo. It's gonna take more muscle and leverage than I've got to budge this door."

We levered the end of the rusty axle between the two doors, each of us grabbing on to help. "Heave-ho!" shouted Tanner, and it began to budge another two inches, but when they peeked inside, it was too dark to see.

"Come on, boys. Give it everything you've got. We'll get her this time."

Suddenly, the heavy timber doors pushed the piled dirt and petrified manure chips aside, exposing the old and unkept stagecoach hidden inside.

"Why she's a monster," I said, slapping my palm on my forehead, surprised. "It looks like it's nearly twice that of the new ones. This old baby looks like she must weigh more than a ton."

"They don't make 'em like they used to." Zeek grinned once they had the door open. "Two thousand two hundred pounds of quality wood and steel. Under that flaked paint is a fine wagon. And here I thought she'd never see the light of day again. I figure the roof protected her from the sun."

"Let's grab the wagon's tongue and pull her out into the main barn so we can get some sunlight on this," Chito-Ochi said. "There's plenty of windows over there. Then we can see exactly what we've got."

"And how are we gonna do that with no back wheels?" I asked the obvious. They all looked, confirming what I said.

I was small enough to fit between all the trash stored against and around the coach. The rear end of the stage was sitting on wooden barrels. Luckily, they had held and hadn't collapsed. The axle was rusty but looked to be whole and in good condition. All it needed was some serious elbow grease.

"No back wheels?" Malvo grumbled, getting cross. "Help me pry that old window open there to the side. It looks like the wood's swelled shut."

After another struggle with the crowbar, we could finally shed some light on our new project. We were greeted with both surprise and disappointment. It was much bigger and built solid, but it was covered in cobwebs, rat and bat poop. They were going to have a job cleaning it up. Of course, there was no time to paint to help disguise it better. On the side doors were remnants of the old Butterfield Stagecoach Company sign, but they were hardly visible. All the metal needed cleaning with a steel brush; a file would do where required.

"That stage must be almost as old as you, Benji," Malvo huffed. "This thing hasn't seen the light of day for years. Still, it looks sturdy enough for what we need if we can get it rolling."

"It does look like she's built mighty solid. I reckon she'll do it after we get her fixed up and roadworthy. All we've got to do is find two sturdy spoked wheels, and we can pull her out." I crawled out of the back, pulled my hat off to dust my clothes, and spat dirt and dried hay from my mouth. Straw poked out from my yellow hair.

"I wouldn't do that if I were you," Marshal Boone said. "If you do the work on this stage anywhere that folks can see ya, the gossip will fly like chaff down a hopper, and any hope of surprise we have will fly out the window."

I looked at my friends one at a time and asked, "Whatcha think we ought to do then? We'll have to put the wheels on, in here if we want to pull her out. I wonder if Mr. Zillow has a couple of spars he can sell us. It looks like all it's missing is that and the rigging, which we can have somebody buy for us in the general store."

"You can pull her into the slot where tomorrow's stage is bedded down. It'll be heading out first thing in the morning. Then you'll have four days to get your work done here before she returns for axle grease and a new team."

Zeek Zillow snickered. It was apparent he thought we were committing a folly, but he also wanted to see the old stage brought back to life.

"I've got two busted wheels I'll give ya for a few bucks, but you'll have to take them to the blacksmith to have him tyre 'em anew. If the metal band is good, hard steel, it'll withstand the weight over the rugged trails you've got ahead."

The work was exhausting, backbreaking, and sometimes dangerous. If a two-thousand-pound wagon fell on you, it was over. If it crushed your leg, it would have to be removed. The thick wooden door swung wide open with a grueling squeak from hinges lacking oil. We continued to work hard in the windless heat as the sun waved in the distance outside. We only left the shed to take a leak and eat, and we never left it with fewer than two men standing guard. All they needed was for a couple of drunken cowboys to stumble upon what we were doing, and the cat would be out of the bag.

The moon was half full and waxing that night as Chito-Ochi's horse walked on eggshells without a sound. As soon as it was dark, he snuck his horse out of the corral, through the barn, and out the back door leading away from Pecos and the city lights. He carefully picked his way, using the moonlight to check for unwanted tracks.

The snort of a pony came from less than a stone's throw away. The Choctaw Indian slipped out of his Indian saddle, and his moccasins silently made puffs of dust rise from the ground. He led his horse by its lead close to the bit-ring, then every few minutes, he would sink to his knees and sniff the air, waiting for a spell before continuing. He watched from a stand of trees and bushes without being discovered. He found nothing alarming as he continued his ride, so he wheeled his horse for the stables.

The Indian scout crept cautiously from cover to cover when a mournful sound cut the stillness. He remained still as a stone until he shook his head and whispered, "Night Birds."

The dark blue of a cloudless night sky was the only redeeming factor of the ragged, wild-looking land. For a second or two, Chito-Oche was a barely visible blur; then, he would disappear into the next shadow, making him almost impossible to detect. His muscles stretched like steel cords with every move. As Chito-Oche looked back, he saw a damp haze blanket the country's flatness.

The Indian brave was wizened and scared with age and battles.

He forced his eyelids to lower slightly until he was peering through bullet-like slits. The moonlight made things waver in the dark. He saw a long shadow run across the distance in a crouch. Then he saw it was a large wolf. Its eyes sown in the dark. It stopped and looked right at him, lingering for a moment before continuing the hunt.

He slipped off his horse and fell to his hands and knees, putting his ear to the ground. Then Chito-Ochi studied the scene stoically beneath impassive eyes. The horse's nose moved softly against his palm, licking his salty perspiration. The Indian whispered into his ear like an old friend.

After a couple of hours, he returned to town. In the dusk, he couldn't see the man's features, but he could make out the silhouette of his revolver on his right leg. When Chito-Ochi got close enough to see who it was, he relaxed. He saw the silhouette of a man with a missing arm. He knew it was Malvo's empty sleeve blowing in the wind.

He was there the day he lost it in the Battle of Sharpsburg, or Antietam, as the Yankees called it. Twenty-two thousand soldiers lost their lives that day, and most of the rest lost their minds. But for the Choctaw Indian, he felt different. Of course, he felt Malvo was his true blood brother, but the other White men, North and South, fought for each other's land. How could he feel for those who wanted to do the same to Choctaw, his own people? So, he wasn't affected in the ways the others were, Malvo included.

Despite looking older, Malvo was only nearing his late twenties. His eyes were beginning to fill with red, but the fire in them belonged to the young man he had been before the war.

The following morning, the first sign of red showed on the skyline, and they knew that in a few minutes, their surroundings would be bathed in light. The four of us worked twenty-four hours a day in shifts, taking three-hour naps after long stretches of grueling work.

I walked up and stood beside my hero and mentor. The granite-faced Indian stared stonily at his young friend and smiled, reaching his eyes. He, too, cared for me, but in a different way than he did for Malvo Tanner. I think he believed I was still moldable, so he could teach the ways of a Choctaw Indian like he would the son he never had. The war stole his youth, so he was too late for some things. But maybe he believed he was given a second chance.

I pushed my hat from my forehead and ran the back of my hand across my mouth. When I spat, it was dry, with little more than dirt and hay. I pulled my handkerchief and blew my nose. It sounded like a horn.

We returned to work, and the marshal came rolling down the street in a borrowed buckboard wagon. He thought it was best *he* took the wheels to be repaired at the blacksmith's because it wouldn't raise as much suspicion as a stranger from the wagon trains. Especially when paying for the hardest and most expensive steel. He said he was doing Zeek a favor, and no more questions were asked. He even gave him a tip for putting the wheel repair at the head of the line of metal objects to make or repair.

In twenty minutes, we had her wheels greased and in place, and we pulled the stagecoach out the shed door and into the main barn. Light spilled into four windows in giant squares, lighting up the whole room. We had brought the old stagecoach back to life.

My curiosity got the best of me, and I couldn't wait to see the inside of the coach. When I first pulled on the stagecoach door, it hardly budged. Then I braced my boots on the only step and put my weight into it. The hinges creaked as the door began to open, and everybody held their breaths. One of the hinges broke under pressure, but it would be easy to fix. When light filled the enclosure, animals scampered from their old home and into the dark corners and up and into the loft. I could hear their little feet scamper as they ran.

I tried to roll up the ancient leather curtains, but they disintegrated in my hands. Surprisingly, the thick leather seats were in good repair. At least they would provide a softer ride, knowing they would be running like the wind.

"Don't worry about the curtains. We won't need them when we're done." Marshal Boone grinned. "When I was in the dump behind the smithy's I saw a half dozen rusted out potbelly stoves, but the doors were in good shape. We can use them to cover the windows. Nobody's gonna get a bullet through one of them."

"They'll make perfect covers for the six windows.

We can hang them on steel hinges so we can close them tight if we need to. That'll take care of us with rifles and shotguns inside. But who's gonna drive the stage?"

"Then we'll have to think of something to protect the driver and the horses," Chito-Ochi said. "I've seen Comanche weave armor for the horses' bodies and necks out of very thick leather. Some of them even made face masks like the Spanish did three hundred years ago when they brought the first horses to our lands. It will stop arrows but won't stop a piece of lead, although it may slow a round down a little. Benji and I can start on them after lunch."

"But what about the driver?" Malvo asked. "I reckon I'm as good a bullwhacker as any, but I'll feel naked sitting out there all alone."

"When we're riding through the day, one of us can spot you with a double-barreled shotgun. I know how to drive a wagon, even if I am an Indian. We can switch so we won't be too worn out if we've got to fight."

"How about if we cut a hole in the front of the coach and run the reins through so if we have to run, we can control the team from inside? The driver and guard can ride outside until we think there'll be trouble." Lem was smarter than the mayor gave him credit for.

"I'll be beside you if we get ambushed, and we should have time to take cover inside. This time, I'll ride out on point every few hours to ensure we don't fall into another trap."

My eyebrows rose as I asked, "What will we do at night?"

"We'll cross that bridge when we get to it." he wiped his forehead with his sleeve and readjusted his eyepatch.

When we finally finished and dared to go outside, we had to squint through the afternoon glare at the end of Main Street. We had been working and sleeping in the barn for three and a half days and were nearly done. We only had twelve hours left before the coach from El Paso returned.

That afternoon, we made an exception and stopped in to see Pedro at the Midnight Saloon. As soon as we walked in, Lem ordered whiskey-dosed coffee all around. We all sat at the marshal's usual table. When I put the tin cup to my lips, the sour taste filled my mouth and nose and burned as I almost gagged and spat it out.

I didn't want whiskey in my coffee, but I didn't want the other men to think I was still a little boy, so I held my breath and took another sip. I tried to hide my sour face and not choke—some of the things you've gotta do when you grow up, I didn't like so much. But riding on our own stagecoach all the way to San Antonio made me laugh every time I thought about it.

I wonder what Junior will do with it when we're done. It would make a grand wagon to live in. Maybe we can use it in our next job too. There's nothing like riding in comfort.

nine
la gran belle

"Whatcha mean that the stagecoach has a name. I've never heard of such a crazy notion." I stared at Zeek, the station owner, like he was crazy. "And what name might that be?"

"Why do you think we call it her? Haven't you ever noticed that all boats and ships have female names written on the stern?"

"What's a stern?"

"It's the flat back of a boat where you'll see a pretty name scrolled across it. It's what folks call a tradition among traveling types. A wagon is nothing more than a boat with wheels. I bet on the Utah salt flats; you could run one with a sail instead of horses. I even brought a bucket of white and gold paint to redo the old Butterfield letters. You might as well advertise for me while you're makin' your journey. It's only fittin' that we christen her with her name again since you've brought her back to life. If you look closely, you'll see remnants of white paint on the back."

"Do we really have to take the time to paint names on our stagecoach right now before we leave? Remember, you *gave* it to us." To me, this still didn't make much sense, but I was beginning to see how much it meant to the waystation owner even if we were in a hurry.

"Exactly, Benji; that's why you should be kind enough to let an aging man have his wish. What harm is it gonna do? I'll do the work myself. I must say, it'll make me feel mighty fine."

"All right, Zeek, we'll do it then." I smiled, but as soon as I opened my mouth, I realized I was out of place speaking for the others, who were all my elders, so I tried to backtrack. "Or at least we might think about making old Mr. Zillow happy. It was a mighty fine gift...the stagecoach, I mean. Sorry if I spoke out of line." I said it with pleading eyes, both for Mr. Zillow's favor and for my judgment error. Now, I was nervous as I waited to face the music, be it good or bad.

I suddenly felt all their eyes on me as the blood drained from my face. I couldn't bring myself to look up, so I stared at my boots and waited to be admonished. I always respected my elders and never talked back or got smart, but I slipped and stuck my foot in my mouth for some reason. If anyone had a say-so in the matter, it would be the man in charge, Malvo or Junior, the owner of the gold and the man who hired us.

For a full minute, everybody was silent. I knew Malvo didn't want to postpone our progress with such an arduous trip ahead. Then, there was the marshal who had known Zeek for much longer than us. I shifted my weight from one foot to the other as nervous energy shot through my body at lightning speed. My stomach suddenly turned over and I felt a little sick. I could feel the sweat pop up on my brow.

"If Benji wants to make Zeek feel better, so do I. Sometimes we Indians name our canoes, too. So, it seems sensible to me. The thing is so big it almost looks like some riverboats I've seen back east." The Choctaw looked at me and winked. It felt good to have my friend back me up.

My sigh of relief was so long that I nearly ran out of air. To my surprise, everybody seemed to like the fact that I showed sympathy and respect for my fellow man and friend, even when I thought I was in trouble for talking out of line. I guess sometimes a fellow must take a chance and speak their mind despite the possible outcomes.

"You're gonna grow up to be a fine young man, Benji Willow." Malvo smiled, showing a mouthful of white teeth as his eyes twinkled with affection. "Well, let's get to it. Daylight's a burnin', and your other stage will be here in the morning. I reckon we shouldn't risk a trial run anyway, even if it is at night. What time is your coach due from El Paso, Zeek?"

"It runs all night on the last stretch because there is no shelter. So, it should arrive around ten o'clock. We'll have to be well clear before then. The horses are gonna come in dead on their feet, and the passengers will be grumpy and hungry. I'll have my hands full all day and probably into the night. It'll light out again the following day to return to El Paso and back. Between that, the next stage will arrive on the southern San Antonio-El Paso run. That's still the way I suggest you take, Malvo."

Tanner nodded. "If there are any outlaws in town, which the marshal is pretty sure there are, they'll expect us to take the northern trail. The Southern Immigrant Trail is a bit longer and has more Indians, but if we become the target of highwaymen, it'll put them off for a few days. Most of them wouldn't bother to cross the south trail for fear of hostiles. I'm countin' on them to thin out the odds. They might not be afraid of us, but they'll be scared of the Comanche and the Apache."

"Benji, you can help your buddy, Zeek," Marshal Boone said. "When you two are done, come over to the Midnight Saloon and have something to eat. We need to get as much food and rest as we can if we're gonna start this long journey tomorrow."

"Once we leave, we won't have much time to rest in between forts," Malvo said, turning on his heels with the others and making a beeline for a drink and a meal.

When we finished the gold letters on both doors, they said BUTTERFIELD STAGECOACH COMPANY. It made the coach look nice, although it did leave the rig appearing older and tattered. On the very back at the top, he painted 'La Gran Belle' in white letters. For some reason, having such a name made me feel like it might bring us luck. Right then, I had no idea what to expect or what the name meant.

"What does her name mean? It's a funny foreign name, ain't it?"

"It means the Great Beauty and that I reckon she is even if she's gettin' old and weathered like me. She's like a graceful lady; she is."

After carefully inspecting his handiwork while blowing on it to help it dry, Zeek stood back a few yards and admired his job. He nodded and smiled. Then we headed for the Midnight Saloon and a much-needed meal. Since I was only fourteen, I ate for two people. I was growing so fast that my bones ached.

"It's about time you two got here. There's your food sitting at the table. I reckon it's cold by now. I never knew it would take so long to paint a few words."

"But you didn't see how pretty it looks, Malvo. The letters on the doors are gold and all. I reckon she looks fine. It's as good a job as I've ever seen by a professional."

I didn't wait another second and grabbed a full pie pan of baked chicken, mashed potatoes, and black beans—that and a half loaf of bread—all washed down with a glass of milk instead of another coffee. At least now, I had learned to pour the coffee, so it came without the dose of whiskey the men insisted on.

"This boy is gonna eat us out of the house and home if we let him. Careful now, and don't get your hands too close to his mouth, or you might find your-self missing a finger." Malvo laughed.

The stagecoach station owner knocked back a glassful of whiskey in one toss as he eyed me and chuckled, but I felt he was laughing with me and not at me. I could see his eyes were already blurry from drink.

Despite the food being cold, I ate all mine and half of Zeek's too. He claimed he wasn't all that hungry, but I knew by his face he enjoyed watching me stuff my face, and there was plenty more where that came from. I ran through every morsel on the table and in record time. When it came time for pie, I had three pieces: that and a whole can of peaches. I don't think I'd ever been that hungry, but then again, I'd never worked day and night for almost a hundred hours with a minimum amount of sleep.

After dinner, as soon as I hit my bedroll on a cushion of hay in Zeek's barn, I didn't move a muscle all night. I was in such a deep sleep that I felt like I was in the depths of a warm, dry cave without a thought or dream bothering me. I slept like a dead man through the night and the wee hours of the morning.

I got up so early it felt like the middle of the night, but I could already hear the odd rooster crow. I had to take a leak, so I tiptoed barefoot across the barn without making a sound. Once I got outside, I saw the moon, claiming it was five o'clock. I knew that within the hour, we would be on our way. I buttoned up and ran for the corral to fetch the horses that we would lead on stringlines. They would be the replacements when the main team got tired.

Chito-Oche straddled his horse and walked it out to the corral, ducking his head as he crossed under the barn door. As the sun came up, he felt the heat rise over his face. He looked out over the countryside with an eye-squinting sternness. He knew what they were heading for more than anyone in the group. The Choctaw and Comanche weren't enemies due to the vast distance between the tribes' locations. Still, due to past encounters, Chito-Oche felt they were personal adversaries because they had slaughtered several of his friends. They were everybody's enemies at times of war and were typically on the warpath.

"Is everybody ready?" Malvo's voice said he was unhurried. He always remained as calm and steady as a rock. He looked around and said, "I thank you kindly, Zeek. Maybe we'll see each other when the marshal returns unless we run into some more work. Things are expensive these days, so we can't sit on our laurels for too long. We never know where our next job is gonna be, but it'll be a fine day when we meet again, old pard."

As the sun rose, light slanted through the open barn doors, making yellow triangles on the floor. Particles of dust floated through the rays, barely visible. Roosters crowed all over the fort and in the chicken coops just outside the log walls as the hens cackled.

We were so drenched in the excitement of the moment that it washed over us, taking away all the nervous tension and any reason to worry about the trip ahead. My skin tingled as a restless urge to move came over me, and I couldn't wait to get underway.

"First, we've gotta store the gold. In these old rigs, Zeek said there's a strongbox built into the floor inside the passenger carriage," Junior huffed.

Until then, he had avoided showing his findings, but as soon as we saw them, we understood their value and the risk we were about to undertake. The Indians would be dangerous as they always were, but American and Mexican outlaws with a taste for gold made for the most ruthless adversaries. The border was only fifty miles south of Chihuahua, a town that dated back to 1709.

Our eyes spread wide when we saw the sacks of gold nuggets as the yellow veins shining in the dazzling morning light. It was the same color as my hair. Some were as big as a melon and many bigger than my fists. Junior grabbed a seat in the passenger compartment and couldn't be pried away from his newfound fortune. He had a thirty-six-inch double twelve-gauges in his already white-knuckled fists. The marshal also rode with his pistols on the seat and a sawed-off ten-gauge shotgun poking out one of the six windows. Now that the bullion was stored, we were ready to let her rip.

"Come on up here with Chito-Ochi and me, Benji. At least for this first stretch of trail." Malvo held the six-horse team's reins, and our Choctaw friend held the whip. "I'm anxious to see how this baby rides after sitting for many years. You should be nice and comfortable inside, Junior. You're in charge of watching your strongbox."

"I doubt anybody could guess what this coach is worth with it full of yellow ore," I said as I climbed the wheel spokes and up to the spring-loaded bench seat.

"I rode out this morning to make sure the first few miles are all clear," the Indian said. "We can ride at ease for the first hour or two as the sun rises. Outside of town, we'll also have a little cool air to start the day."

We looked out at the climbing, stretching, never-ending flatness before us. The horses moved into a quickly ending gloom. The dimness clung close to the ground, but soon, the sun climbed higher, shooing away the shadows and burning away the mist. Suddenly, we were off, bouncing down the street at a neck-breaking pace. Malvo intended for the stagecoach to remain visible for the shortest time possible as we headed for a cross street and the end of town.

Our horses' hooves pounded hard-packed dirt and rock as the wheels corkscrewed dust in circles, accumulating into a cloud so thick behind us that we couldn't see if anyone was following. But that meant that from behind, nobody could see us either.

In the Choctaw's expert hand, the bullwhip cracked over the horses' heads as we raced across the narrow street at a gallop. When we turned the corner at the edge of town, the stagecoach almost skidded sideways on the loose stones and into a haberdashery. We careened too close to the boardwalk, tilting up on two wheels until the horses found solid ground and the stage righted itself. Malvo pointed the team toward the end of Pecos and relative safety along the well-traveled road.

A hint of a smile softened the straight lips of Malvo's mouth. I pulled my coat tight across my shoulders against the early morning desert chill.

Junior sat inside. His old face was scared, with crow's feet stretching around the corners of his eyes and deep lines across his brow. His skin was like worn leather.

We could only hear the rumbling sound of the wagon's wheels and the pounding of the horses' hooves, making us shout to speak. I could hear the crack of reins slapping the backs of the six-horse team. The ponderous creaking of wooden-spoked and iron-rimmed wheels was followed by circles of dust that appeared to turn backward.

By the end of the first day, Junior's sunburned face showed through his scraggly beard as he stepped out of the carriage covered in dust. It was too hot inside to leave the cast-iron window down. We all had our hats pushed back and were dirty and tired.

Malvo and Chito-Oche stretched, pushing their fists into the small of their backs. They stood there deep in thought, staring at their boots, each wondering what the following days would bring. The marshal spat out the stub of a cigar and crushed it with his boot heel.

"It looks like we've got to stop here for the night to give the animals the rest. If not, this heavy stagecoach will wear them out before we hit our next stop in Fort Stockton. If we don't kill the horses on the way, we should be there by sundown tomorrow. That will lead us to Edwards Plateau." Tanner spat a stream of brown juice onto the ground.

"What's the next stop after that, Malvo?"

"That'll be Fort McKavett in Sonora. That's another one hundred seventy miles right through land the Indians claim as theirs. That should damper the intentions of most outlaws after what they might think is in the stage."

The horses' lungs were worn out, so they breathed

through their mouths. They stood wavering in the heat and dust, their heads down. They had to be careful not to push them too hard. Even the spare team was tired.

As soon as it was dark, Chito-Ochi ran half-crouched even though there was no moon, and he could hardly see. He moved using his instincts and years of war experience with little more to guide him. He stopped for a moment and pressed flat against the trail with his ear to the ground, holding his breath and listening. His heart pounded between his ears, but nobody was close enough to hear. He believed they could ride for half a day without mishap—hopefully longer.

We unhooked the horses and ground-tied them near some grass. They grazed, sliding their jaws and whisking their tails as they flicked their ears against flies. That night, my eyes glowed orange as I stared into the fire. It was the end of July in this part of the country, with eighty-to-ninety-degree days and cool nights.

"Do you think we'll run into any Indians?" My voice cracked. I didn't sound as confident as I'd hoped.

"Are you the kind of fella that walks under a flock of birds and doesn't expect to get crap on your face?" Malvo chuckled. "I reckon Indians, in these parts, especially Comanche, are the order of the day. With this iron wagon, we might be able to keep the hostiles at bay, but it's the determined outlaws that I'm concerned about: both white and brown."

A dozen falling stars left vapor trails streaking toward Earth and then burned out in midair. Minutes later, the sky burst into a pink, rose, and crimson prism as it stretched to the western horizon.

Stillness held heavy over the men sitting in the grove. Tin cups clinked, and then dust-covered boots scraped the ground. The campfire in the center died in a puff of smoke. Junior stretched stiffly on his bedroll. He yawned so wide they could almost see his stomach.

men of reckless blood

When we raced out of Pecos, people ran onto the street to see the spectacle. Rumors were already rampant. By the end of the fourth day, every local knew something was happening inside the Butterfield Stage barns. Still, the whole town was surprised when the massive old coach roared out the large doors and down the street, careening to one side, nearly tipping over, as it raced around corners like a duck with its tail on fire. The cracks of the whip sounded like six-shooters going off as the massive wheels raced for the other end of the street.

The original idea was to get out of town quickly with as few spectators as possible, but that plan failed miserably. The local merchants noted all the supplies purchased and assumed they were rigging a new wagon. From one day to the next, it was the talk of the town. None of them expected the La Gran Belle to come roaring out of the carriage house doors after so many years. The news sped across the city nearly as fast as the stage, racing down the streets toward the southeast exit and the southern road to San Antonio.

The temporary visitors to Pecos often outweighed the registered residents. Cowboys, overlanders, and men of ill intent came by the hundreds and added to the crowds as the town overflowed with strangers from other parts. Among those were outlaws from both north of the Rio Grande and south of the border. Greed for gold required no specific race or color. Some outlaws said gold coins didn't have owners, only spenders, and to the strong goes the spoils.

Even a couple of bands of half-breeds blessed Pecos due to its proximity to the Mexican border and possible escape. These men were rejected by the white, red, or brown and, due to their circumstances, almost always turned to crime.

Some of these men of reckless blood had done their homework, too. They had spies in the bank where the bounty hunters chased their checks, so they knew who they were and why they were so well paid. Malvo Tanner and Chito-Ochi were among the most dangerous man-hunters in the state, so they all knew that they would have to approach cautiously.

But if their suspicions were correct and they were taking gold or silver to San Antonio, they were prepared to do whatever it took to make themselves rich. When the yellow mineral came into the equation, even weak men became brave and took risks they would normally never take.

As the end of another day came, the sun neared the end of the world. We finally arrived at the watering hole marked on Zeek's map to refresh the horses. When we stopped, we saw a thin line of gray smoke in the distance as it spiraled high into the sky. Chito-Och climbed down from the stage and pulled a handful of grass, letting it fall to indicate the direction of the wind. The blades of grass drifted toward the smoke.

"What is it?" He was making me nervous, especially as darkness was nearing. I watched as he studied our surroundings.

Chito-Ochi moved all around the watering hole, his nose inches from the ground. He stopped and picked up a dirt clod, breaking it open and smelling it, too. Then he dropped it, only to search for another and do the same.

"Two horses and riders," my Choctaw friend replied. He took a deep whiff of dirt and tossed it to the ground.

"Are they Indians?" I couldn't keep the worry from my voice.

Chito-Ochi shook his head. "Men wear boots, and horses have shoes. I've seen one of these fellas before."

"How can you possibly know such a thing?"

"One of his boot heels is cracked." He pointed with his finger. "Can you see it now? Same boot, same man. I saw that footprint back near the stagecoach station in Pecos."

"Are they doggin' us?" Malvo asked.

"Yes, but these two are only scouts sent out ahead. There will be more of them somewhere out there. Soon, it will be dark, and we can go and see where they're camped. Only then will we know their numbers although we can assume their intentions."

When I saw the horses walk away from the water, I asked, "Why don't the horses drink from the pond?"

"The same reason we won't. See those antlers sticking out of the water over there? The outlaws blocked the stream so the water wouldn't flow and poisoned it with rotten meat. Empty the water bags, or we'll all get sick. Zeek marked another place on the map not too far away. Without his notes, we'd be up a creek without water *or* paddle."

"Malvo and I will have to swing around so they're upwind, or their horses will smell ours and nicker or neigh, giving us away along with our approximate location. You three stay here well-armed inside the wagon and hold the fort down until we return. We've gotta find out who those men are and confirm if they're looking for us or not. If anybody but us gets near the coach while we're gone, shoot 'em if they show the slightest aggression. This is not the time to hesitate. Anybody who shows up here at night is unwelcome because they're up to no good."

As I watched Chito-Ochi, I realized there was much more to Indian knowledge than I ever imagined. My Choctaw friend seemed to know the earth's secrets—things unknown to White men. While Lem, Junior, and I unhitched the horses, brushed them down, and made sure they were properly fed, we waited for our leaders to return. No matter where we were or who we were with, Malvo always seemed to be in charge, and nobody ever contested his authority.

Maybe they knew his worth, or maybe they knew better.

The bounty hunters swung wide around the stream of smoke now barely visible in the darkening sky. They made out four men and two tents when they got close enough to see their faces before the campfire. Eight horses were tied to ground stakes as they grazed, pulling tufts of grass and sliding their jaws.

Right after they heard someone with a gruff voice complain in English, they saw the ten-flap open, and an ex-soldier emerged. He wore the remnants of a Union officer but looked more like an outlaw or killer than the soldier he might have once been. Before hooking his wire-rimmed spectacles around his ears, he cleaned them with the tail of his shirt. He dusted the dirt off his clothing with his hat and brushed his mustache with his knuckles.

Back at the stage, I boasted, "They wouldn't dare mess with us," but my voice didn't convey the confidence I wanted. I closed my eyes and listened like Chito-Ochi did, but all I heard was the moan of the wind.

"Here, put a dash of this in your coffee," Marshal Boone said as he uncorked the whiskey jug and poured a splash into my tin cup. When I took a sip, I spilled the liquor nervously and then wiped my chin with the heel of my hand. Everything was so exciting; it was palpable. It made me want to pee.

"Truth is a byproduct of a man's character," Marshal Boone pondered like he was telling me the secrets of life. "Honest men reveal their truths with every breath they take. But dishonest men distort the same."

Every day I was with the marshal, the more I liked him. He seemed rough and gruff back in town, but we all traveled as friends on the trail. Clearly, he saw Malvo as an equal, if not a man of superior knowledge and skills. Still, there was obviously no jealousy between any of us. Not even with all of Junior's gold at stake. Sure, we all looked forward to healthy paychecks, but that was enough to placate us for our need for money to survive. Luckily for us, we always had more work. I somehow believed that my friends' interest in wealth was nearly nonexistent as they wouldn't know what to do with so much gold even if it was theirs.

A couple of hours later, when it was completely dark inside the stage, we heard something like a key rattle in a lock. Then came the sound of scratching on the stagecoach door. I blinked like a bird as I looked at Marshal Boone with questioning eyes.

The Pecos lawman put his finger to his lips and mouthed, "Shush." My blood chilled when we heard something scuffling in the dirt outside the carriage. Lem had a Colt-45 revolver in each hand.

We ducked lower to the floor and out of sight, so in the dark, it made us nearly impossible to see. Just then, a red, hairless face looked right into the stage window, but as we lay as still as church mice, he didn't see us looking back. I held my pa's heavy Colt Walker in two hands with my thumb on the hammer as beads of sweat ran down my face. It suddenly dawned on me that I'd never shot a man in the face at point-blank range.

The first Comanche that I'd seen up close had streaks of ochre and brown painted down his face from top to bottom, making him blend in with his surroundings. He also carried a six-shot pistol in his hand and a bow and quiver of arrows across his back. When he looked at where we were hiding, we froze. For a moment, I knew that I would soon be scalped, or he would be dead; I remember what Malve had said. Then, his eyes continued to graze across the distance and away from the passenger compartment. He was obviously a scout. His drapes of black hair fluttered in the wind as he remounted.

Finally, he wheeled his pony west silently and broke into a long lope. I don't think I breathed until I saw his shadow diminish, along with the soft sound of his pony's unshod hooves. Soon, there wasn't a trace of the intruder, and I gulped and gobbled air along with Junior and Lem. All our eyes were spread wide as concern etched across our faces. We hadn't been much more than three feet from the Comanche warrior. The hair on the back of my neck stood on end, and I felt war drums beating in my chest. I ran my tongue over my cracked, dry lips.

When Malvo and Chito-Ochi returned, I could hardly keep my eyes open from bouncing around after an exhausting day on the stage. The tension of the Comanche also took its toll, as stress drained the rest of my energy, making my eyes heavy.

That morning, a blue haze surrounded the glare as we stared farther across the distance. In some places, the road was in good repair, and others were full of potholes, bad batches, and trench-like ditches from thousands of wagon wheels of the settlers and miners heading for California. One of the horses screamed as the others began pawing the ground, neighing shrilly and straining at their dancing reins.

"I believe that Comanche Indian you saw was a forward scout for a war party roaming around out there somewhere. Now, I reckon those four outlaws we discovered are doggin' our trail. They've made the mistake of following us upwind. That's what made our horses squeal. Now that we know they're behind us, whatcha wanna do, Malvo?"

"For now, let's act like we don't know they're there. That will give us the advantage of surprise. Then, when we see our chance, Chito-Ochi and I can end their mission, and if they resist, maybe their lives."

While I was riding inside the coach on soft, cushy seats, I studied Junior. He was lean and beginning to become slightly stooped, humping his back when he sat. He claimed before that he wore a raccoon cap, but with age, he favored flat-brimmed Stetsons that provided plenty of shade from the Texan sun. He had been heading for the California gold fields when he stopped in West Texas and appeared to get stuck. It seemed like he always found just enough gold in his pan to keep his hopes up, and for twenty years, he mined the area. His scraggly hair hung to his shoulders, and his tangled beard to his belly.

When it started to rain, it sounded like little bullets on the stage's wooden roof. Of course, it was void of luggage because all our meager personal possessions were in the passenger carriage. Then, there was a downpour for five minutes, leaving small water puddles as far as the eye could see as clouds reflected on the surfaces. The rain finally wore itself out and turned into a warm drizzle. Chito-Ochi's wet muscles rippled up and down his arms and back. The veins in his neck looked like mooring lines, ridged and hard.

Malvo and Chito-Ochi relished the shower as they opened their mouths, sticking their tongues out and filling them with fresh water. It came down so hard that their hats began to droop, but it was still hot inside. We rode through the day with the men driving the stage, always carefully tracing the trail for signs of horses and footprints, meaning trouble.

At midday, we saw where numerous hoofprints marred the wet earth. A war party had been there before us. After us, we knew the outlaws would come. Now everything was soft and muddy as steam hissed from the warm ground. My guts turned to ice water, and I went rigid like an ice sickle when I thought about being between the two like a poison sandwich. As I waited, I began to shudder like a feather in a windstorm, and my mouth was as dry as a corn bin after a drought.

This time, Tanner left his friend to the reins as he rode out a mile or two to see if he could locate the small war party. Their prints said they were traveling the same way as us. Malvo's 50-caliber Sharps rifle lay across his lap as he searched for the perfect place for someone to hide for an ambush.

Tanner slapped his rifle's stock against his horse's

rump, breaking into a lope to see what he could find. Swinging from a clearing, he zigzagged through scattered cacti while loosely guiding his horse's reins. He was sure that the small war party was out front, and the four men trailing us were somewhere not too far away.

We continued our way with Chito-Ochi at the reins and the marshal and me riding shotgun on top. My gut feeling told me it was just a matter of time. The marshal exhaled a blast of cigarette smoke as he wiped the sweat from his brow. His eyes were full of tension as he clenched his teeth, ready in a moment to fire his gun.

Finally, the sun suddenly came from over the horizon like a big red rubber ball, stretching its light rays across the countryside.

A voice seemed distant as it came from outside the stagecoach. "Drop your guns, boys: you're surrounded.".

We looked just in time to see four men on horses riding at a long lope, and they had revolvers in their fists. That was when we heard the deep discharge of the Sharps buffalo gun. The bullet slammed into the closest man, throwing him five yards to the ground. The only sound was a whimper as he struggled for one last gasp of air. He had a bullet hole in his chest just above his sternum. The three remaining outlaws scattered as though the blast was the starter at a horse race, heading back from where they came, but Malvo was waiting.

The blast of a scattergun went off nearby. The first barrel knocked two men off their horses. Malvo dropped his rifle and pulled his pistol like he had all the time in the world. He seemed to shoot without even aiming, but the bullet found its target right between his eyes. The two men full of buckshot moaned as they wriggled on the ground.

"Are there any more of your gang members out there?" Tanner growled. "Speak up, and I'll put you two out of your misery. You're gonna die right here anyway. You can go quick or slow; take your pick."

"We ain't in no gang. We heard you had a wagon full of gold. We're just poor cowboys lookin' to get ahead."

That was the last thing the young buckaroo said before he died. His friend followed him ten minutes later. Despite the threat, Malvo didn't have it in him to shoot a man who was already down.

"You don't scare easily, do you, Benji?" Marshal Boone asked.

"I doubt I really had time to be scared. When it's all said and done, it is when I get nervous and maybe a little frightened. That and right before it happens if I have time to think about it, which I usually don't."

The marshal leaned back, stretching his suspenders with his thumbs, and his eyes twinkled like little stars. "It looks like we made it through our first problem. I wonder what that Comanche war party is up to."

The outlaws had hesitated. Malvo's sudden appearance knocked them off balance, and now all four were dead. They had let greed take over their common sense, and now they wouldn't be herding any more cattle.

fort mckavett

Before Fort McKavett was established, a civilian community was present a mile to the north. Scabtown was founded by a German merchant named Lehnesburg, but the name didn't stick. Upon the arrival of US Army troops in 1852, it was first called San Saba because it overlooked the San Saba River Valley and eventually became Fort McKavett.

It was placed there to protect the frontier settlers and overlanders on the southern San Antonio-El Paso Road. Its hilltop position gave them a strategic advantage, providing distant views in all directions. Water springs and game were abundant in the area, so they could easily feed the soldiers.

Pecan and oak trees provided the lumber to build the fort, and quarried stones were used to construct the buildings. By road, the journey to San Antonio was two hundred seventy-one miles, ninety miles north of the Mexican border.

As soon as we reached the last stretch of land before

the fort, which we could see on a hill in the distance, we saw the first tracks of the Comanche. Chito-Ochi came racing for the stage, waving his rifle over his head, screaming, "Drive the horses as hard as you can! The valley is alive with hostile Indians!"

Little did they know two hundred fifty Comanche warriors had descended on the valley and had already murdered several of the ranchers nearby. As we raced for the fort, we passed the Dawson ranch, where an unsettling scene was already taking place, just a mile and a half from safety.

They saw a White man who gave them a hint of what was to come. His body was stripped naked; his back was riddled with puncture wounds from knives, spears, and arrows. A single bullet hole went from his back to the front of his throat. His clothing was wet, suggesting he tried to swim across the San Saba in a desperate bid for an unsuccessful attempt to escape.

I looked on in horror, even though I had seen worse. "Why didn't they scalp him, Chito-Ochi?" I asked, but he shrugged and shook his head.

We saw another body speared with a long lance. It had pierced her spine, severing it along with several ribs. She was a pretty young girl, just about my age. From the tracks, hundreds of Indians stormed the ranch house. Furniture littered the yard, where mattresses were hacked to pieces, leaving thousands of white feathers floating in the breeze. Dishes and clothing lay abandoned, and the corals were empty.

"Maybe they saw the women run for the house, and their interest was drawn away from the poor soul they killed by the river. That's the only reason I can see that he wasn't scalped. Back there, I saw the tracks of well over two hundred Indian ponies herding ten heads of thousand cattle. We can't stop and help the dying, or we'll be next. We've gotta make a mad dash for Fort McKavett."

Malvo stood as he lashed the reins on the team's backs and yelled until his voice gave out. I sighed deeply when we saw the fort gates, but panic struck me when I noticed they were closed. I wondered if the soldiers would open fire on us out of desperation. It was obvious there was a Comanche uprising happening right before our eyes. We walked out of the skillet and right into the fire.

"Put this white cloth on the end of the whip, Marshal, and hang it out the window so they know we're friendly," Malvo yelled. "Otherwise, we might end up full of holes. Everybody is gonna be as nervous as hell, and that makes men trigger-happy.

"As soon as the soldiers saw the peace flag, they real-ized the old stagecoach and its occupants racing for the fort were White men, not Comanche. As we were nearly on top of the fort, the massive log gates swung open just wide enough for us to race in. They were swiftly closed behind us, and a large beam was laid across the width of the entrance, locking the gates in place.

"What in the world are you fellas doin' out there? We're under a full Comanche attack. We've sent runners to Mason and Camp San Saba for reinforce-ments to give them notice that they should remain in their homes at the risk of losing their lives. Now, we've got two cavalry companies scouting for frontier posts a few hours' ride from here, and they don't know what's happening. Somehow, we've got to notify them to return to the fort forthwith, or we risk losing all those men."

"Do you have a fast, fresh horse?" Chito-Ochi asked.

Both Malvo and I looked at our best friend like he must be mad after barely making it to safety with the stage.

"Whatcha mean, Chito-Ochi? You don't plan to go back out there on your own, do you?" My voice was full of doubt.

"We've got the captain's racehorse. It's the fastest horse on the San Saba River." The soldier looked at the Choctaw Indian with pleading eyes. "If you could ride all night, you should get there before hostiles hit them."

Our friend sat on a wild-looking stallion. In minutes, prancing and pulling at the bit, the mighty stallion was ready to run, even before the gate opened. Chito-Ochi dug his heels into the black beauty's flanks and shot out of the two-yard opening like a Chinese rocket on the Fourth of July. A dust cloud followed in his wake. I'd never seen such a fast horse.

Malvo climbed down from the stage's driver's seat and shook his head. "I wonder what got into him, flaunting death like that."

As the sun sat squat on the world's rim, the night began to recapture the day the Choctaw Indian rode into the dark. He carefully traveled as quickly as possible all night, dodging Comanche war parties and scouts, arriving at first light the following morning.

A camp full of army tents lay peacefully beside Spring Creek, obviously unaware of the uprising, which surprised the messenger. He had seen several smaller war and scouting parties during the night to raise the alarm. Chito-Ochi believed if they pulled up stakes and made haste, they could return to the fort before the Comanche located them. It was evident that they had yet to discover their presence, or they would have turned and run by now.

"Fort McKavett is surrounded. Ranches across the countryside have been attacked, and their large herds run off. Captain Walter Riley said that you and your men should return to help to fight off the assailants and save yourselves." Chito-Oche gobbled air, nearly out of breath. "Sergeant Cassidy gave me the captain's horse, which I believe you probably recognize."

"You should feel yourself lucky you didn't get shot when you rode holus-bolus into our camp. Of course, I recognized the captain's famous racing horses, or *you*, mister, would be a dead man."

"Do you want me to wait and help guide you through the roaming war parties? We can use the same route I rode last night. My loaned horse doesn't seem hardly tired, something that I can't say for myself."

"Why, we're out here hunting Indians, Fool. Do you think we're here or the fun of it? If these Indians want to be whipped, let them come and get us. Just point me in their direction."

"Everywhere between here and Fort McKavett and

probably north and south of that. There are hundreds of them, and they're armed to the teeth. On our way into the fort, we saw about two hundred fifty braves on the warpath. The farms and ranches around the fort are already burned to the ground, the cattle stolen, the settlers dead or dying. This is as serious as it gets, Lieutenant."

"I'll have my men mount up and go search for them forthwith."

"Don't worry, you won't have to look for them. They'll find *you* soon enough. I can guarantee you that."

The soldiers looked tired and had curious eyes. The wrinkles in their faces were dirt-creased, and they all had a week's beard. Their ill-fitting uniforms, with buttons missing, were covered in fine dust. Rifles were slung across their backs, and the two officers and a sergeant carried Colt Patterson revolvers. Only the officer in charge looked immaculate, wearing a full uniform with polished brass buttons.

It looked like Chito-Ochi's plea for salvation was going to go unanswered. The army-sized companies were each composed of sixty calvary men. Their commanding officer seemed unfazed and disregarded the warning. The blood lust was in his eyes for anyone to see.

I bet he's never even been in a fight with the Comanche, or he wouldn't be in such a rush, the Choctaw Indian thought.

"So, you mean to tell me I rode all this way, risking my life for nothing? I thought you'd value your men more than that. These are the most dangerous Indians in the West, but I reckon you've already been told that."

"That was your poor choice, mister. Like I said, you were lucky we didn't shoot you on sight." The lieutenant forced a smile, but it didn't reach his dead-cold eyes, which were full of fight.

"Two regular companies of a hundred twenty men won't do much against two hundred fifty Comanche warriors with modern rifles. It looks like half of your men are new troopers. This raid looks to be well planned. These men have been fighting for decades. That's a lot longer than we fought in the Civil War, and they know the land like the back of their hands. Are you sure I can't change your mind, sir?"

Seeing how the officer looked down his nose at him and his effort was unwanted, without another word, Chito-Oche wheeled his horse around and clicked his tongue, and the black stallion shot off like a bullet despite having run all night. The Choctaw Indian was so exhausted he weaved in the saddle for most of the day, but again, he avoided the onslaught of Comanche across the countryside. All four of us were waiting on the wall-walk when we saw the black stallion running toward the fort in the distance.

"Open up the gates, quick. We have one of our men coming in hot!" Malvo yelled.

Behind Chito-Ochi rode twenty Comanche warriors, riding as fast as they could. We heard gunshots in the distance, but they weren't in Winchester range yet. The Indians must have been shooting rounds into the air to scare their opponents, but my friends didn't scare easily.

"Is she loaded, Benji? Malvo asked as I passed him his buffalo gun. He carefully laid the barrel on a bedroll at the top of the fort's wall.

"How far out do you make the lead rider, Marshal?"

"They're still too far away, Malvo. I'd say about a thousand yards."

The gun's boom surprised the marshal as he jumped an inch off the walkway. To his surprise, the first horse's knees buckled as it skidded and toppled over, trapping the rider underneath its body.

"Damn, that was one hell of a shot." Boone removed his hat, wiped his brow with his sleeve, and used it to block the sun.

As soon as Malvo fired, I passed him Chito-Ochi's buffalo gun, already loaded. Boom! The Sharps roared. Flame and smoke followed the lead bullet out of the barrel, closing the distance between the enemy some eight hundred yards out.

Even from such a distance, he looked like he was hit in the chest with a sledgehammer. The Comanche warrior flew off the back of the horse and tumbled to the ground, as his mount continued to run. The horse right behind it was hit by the same bullet that passed through the first Comanche. It began to stagger from side to side, trying to stay upright, but as it slowed, it lay down, as blood ran from its mouth.

A third and a fourth shot followed with the same results. When they got into Winchester rifle range,

Marshal Booneand I opened up, making sure we shot wide of our friend as he raced to safety. The Sharps slowed their charge until they finally veered off to fight another day. Chito-Ochi roared through the fort gates as they slammed shut behind him. Now, me and a dozen soldiers opened fire, too. Then, all the Indians escaped over a rise in the land and disappeared as quickly as they had appeared.

To our disbelief, five minutes later, four riders led four riderless ponies onto the battlefield, knowing well they could get cut down like their friends. Booneraised his rifle, but Malvo grabbed the barrel, pushing it down.

"That's enough needless bloodshed for one day. Hopefully, there won't be any more. They just wanna come and collect their dead and give them proper burials. We can't deny them that, can we."

I saw the captain coming our way out of the corner of my eye. "I was watching at the other end of the wall-walk with my field glasses when you shot that Indian from a thousand yards out, Malvo. I've never seen such a shot." He slapped his leg and laughed. "Bully for you, Mr. Tanner. You too, young man. I bet you'd make me a fine soldier."

"Benji works for me, and the marshal here works for the state. Everybody is suddenly offering us jobs." Malvo chuckled, too. It was good to be alive.

"How about the Choctaw Indian scout? Does he work for you, too? I could use more men like you fellows."

"Chito-Ochi is my business partner; before that, he

was my spotter in the Civil War. We're inseparable, sir. Good men are hard to find, ain't they."

"Let's climb down from here and find out what your partner saw during the last twelve hours. Since he made it back, I believe he'll know more about what's happening on the ground than us."

When Chito-Ochi told the captain exactly what his lieutenant said, word for word, I found his recklessness hard to believe myself.

Captain Walter Riley stood momentarily, chewing on what he just heard. "If that dammed fool lieutenant gets my soldiers killed, I'll court-martial him. Did you tell him these were my orders, Chito-Ochi? You're a brave man for what you did. Were you one of my soldiers, I'd give you a medal. Just remember, if you ever need a job, there's one here waiting for you."

A hint of a smile tugged at the edges of his mouth as he nodded in recognition. Chito-Ochi didn't like people doting on him for doing his job. Instead, he just stood there as stiff as a statue. Only Malvo knew how uncomfortable he was. An old dust-covered dog barked dispiritedly and lazily crawled under the captain's porch.

"Livin' in West Texas is a lot riskier than growin' corn in Oregon, ain't it, Benji."

"The Panhandle up on the Red River wasn't a piece of cake, either. In my short life, there's one thing I've learned. Everywhere you find Comanche, you'll find violence."

Captain Riley smelled of duty and honor. The marshal gave him a dubious look. He knew how the law really worked and how many wicked men lived this far west. He believed that most officers who came to distant forts in the Territories were looking for fame and glory but usually found the bitter truth; something they had never imagined.

The fact was that they were fighting a war to eliminate a race of people and not enjoy some wealthy man's sport. The marshal struggled to mask his frustration and contempt. He imagined the captain came from a wealthy Northern family and hadn't suffered the hardships he and his friends had.

"You did some fine shooting for such a young man. You know how to handle you, Winchester, I'll say that."

The captain could see the light in my eyes grow brighter with the compliment. I even unconsciously jutted out my chin and puffed up my chest in response. I felt almost manic with excitement. I fantasized about doing all the things my two best friends had done. Right then, I knew riding with Mr. Tanner and Chito-Ochi was the best choice I had ever made. To be complimented by a captain from the frontier forts, no less, was more than I ever expected.

"Let's go have us something to settle our nerves. Drinks are on me," the captain said. "Scouting is thirsty work, Benji. Sometimes, you end up hot, hungry, freezing and tired all at the same time. I reckon I've rattled on long enough and maybe more than I should have. I know that you have had your own hard times. Especially crossing the Oregon Trail and after. Malvo told me what happened to you and your family up on the Southern Red River."

Despite the marshal's obvious distaste, the captain seemed to have taken a shine to me, and I liked him anyway. For being such an important officer, he seemed like an honest and fair man, unlike some of the soldiers we encountered, especially those from the North.

"I fought my share of Indians back on our way down the Chisholm Trail," Junior reminisced. He detailed the sheer terror of the Indian raids. "They were the lords of the plains before the White men came, you know. I'll never forget them whooping their war cries and firing their rifles and bows like demons from the apocalypse."

Regardless of the violent nature of his tales, Junior's eyes came alive with excitement despite the obvious terror he had suffered. As old memories were rekindled, the fire in his eyes glowed like red-hot cinders.

I nodded, picturing the charred ruins of my family's ranch house. I remember it all too well. All those hours stuck down there in that hole, not knowing what would happen, burned in my brain like a branding iron.

When they entered the fort saloon, the compound soldiers all stepped forward, offering their hands. Everyone liked the Choctaw Indian, even though they really didn't know him. Still, he had risked his life for men like them and did so without hesitation.

The aging Junior smiled, showing his tobacco-stained teeth. After squinting momentarily, he spat a long stream of brown juice into the spittoon, making it ring as his eyes shined.

"If you don't make your life purposeful, you risk declining into vice and violence," Marshal Boone growled. He was acting like he did back in Pecos, putting up a shield to warn strangers not to get too close. Luckily, I knew him better than that.

bar room fight

When Malvo walked into the saloon, he stopped, framed in the doorway, a silhouette in the morning light. Everybody turned our way. It was almost like they felt it when he entered. The captain waved his open hand and showed the way, guiding us to his personal table. A picture window provided the best view of the main grounds outside of the saloon.

I was surprised when I saw how rowdy the fort's saloon was. Having just met the captain, I believed everywhere would be neat and orderly, and the men respectful of their head officer. But although it was clear that they loved their captain, his soldiers were as rowdy as the cowboys back in Pecos. Some of them yelled and threatened each other, but I didn't know if they were in earnest or not.

Even though we got lots of backslaps and recognition for how we had helped, there was a sergeant who sat in the corner eyeing us with calculating, cold eyes. It didn't look like he was impressed, even by Chito-Ochi's bravery when confronting the Comanche to warn his fellow men. I knew the soldiers would be scared to death when facing the Texas tribes, but their officers were constantly rotated in and out, and most of them were looking for trophies. It was the same across the thirteen forts on the Texan frontier.

"Why, I bet Malvo is the best shot in Texas. What else are you good at, Mr. Tanner?" the captain continued to dote on his new visitors. "I could swear that first heathen was a thousand yards away when you shot his horse. I would have never thought of that and would have aimed for the Indian."

"He can Indian wrestle better than me, too." Chito-Ochi smiled at his partner, knowing that Malvo hated the attention.

"Are you a boxing fan, Malvo?" the captain asked.

"I've been known to a round of fisticuffs a time or two. Out here, we don't fight like folks do back in the East. The only rules we have in bare knuckle fights this far west are no guns or knives."

"We have regular competitions here at the fort. It helps the men blow off steam and settle disagreements," the captain added. "For us, it's all in fun, though. I make all the men shake hands before they head for their bunks. All this makes for a stronger bond among the men."

"After chasing Comanche all day, a man *does* get worked up and needs a way to blow off some steam. I can vouch for that myself," Malvo replied. "When we first met, Chito-Ochi and I would occasionally have a go at each other. Back then, we were just workin' on bein' friends. I reckon that's one of the reasons we became such good business partners. He's more like a brother to me. We've been riding together for so long, I don't know what I'd do without him."

"How about you try out our Sergeant Bones, Mr. Tanner?" a private called out from a table nearby. "He's been the fort's champion for the last three years. Hostiles killed the only soldier who ever beat him, but it took three of them to do it. Or is all that reputation you carry around for fun? Whatcha say?"

"Mr. Tanner didn't come here to fight with my men. Why, we've only just met. I'd hate for us to get started on the wrong foot. But it is true about Leroy. The big Scotsman has beaten every man that challenged him but one, and he was twice your size. I'd hardly say it would be a fair fight for my sergeant to duke it out with you. I don't feel it would be an even match. No offense intended, Malvo."

I wasn't sure I knew what I was hearing. I never heard of friends fighting for fun unless they were brothers. I used to punch it out with my twin, James. Even though we got mad, we never meant to hurt each other. I sat on pins and needles, wondering if Malvo would take the bait and, if he did, would win.

I had seen him fight with guns, knives, and even bows and arrows, but a bare-knuckled fistfight somehow didn't seem right. From what Chito-Ochi told me, Malvo fought like an Indian and not so much like the Americans or English I've read about in the dime novels. They stood up straight, twirling their fists.

I couldn't even imagine Malvo doing that, especially with one hand.

Somebody released a shrill whistle from the saloon door, and then I heard more men running. Everybody wanted to see the fight. Sergeant Bones had quite a reputation, but some of the soldiers had read about the bounty hunters, too. Now, the room was tense, waiting to see if Malvo Tanner would stand against their champion. The tension in the room was so heavy I could hardly breathe.

"I don't fight one-armed men, especially when they're missing an eye. How about the Choctaw Indian, and I have a go at it? He seems more my type." Leroy said, puffing out his chest and growling to intimidate.

We could see in his face that the sergeant loved to fight.

"So, now you're gonna sit there and insult me to my face?" Malvo growled.

All the while, his expression was an impossible mask to read.

"Because I'm missing bits and pieces, do you think you're more of a man than I am?"

"Nobody is trying to insult you, Malvo," the captain interjected, then turned to his sergeant. "Don't get out of line, Leroy. You know I don't like smart alecks."

"Leave 'em go, Captain. He's a grown man. Let him decide," the challenger snarled.

I was surprised when Chito-Oti chuckled. It

appeared he was enjoying the little exchange. I noticed that nobody seemed to be afraid.

"All right, then, One-Eye," Sergeant Bone beckoned. "If you think you're so bad, let's see whatcha got. Don't expect me to go easy on ya either. You asked for it. So, I ain't gonna hold back."

Leroy began unbuttoning his shirt, stripping down to navy-blue long johns. Malvo slowly laid his hat on the table, removed his Navy Colts, and pulled off his shirt. His stump was cut off four inches below the elbow and scarred. To everybody's surprise, he removed his boots and socks and passed them to me.

"Watch my silver spurs, Benji, and wish me luck. That sergeant looks like a mean critter, doesn't he?"

I opened and closed my mouth like a goldfish in a fishbowl, not knowing how to reply. "Good luck, then," I said feebly, blinking my eyes.

By the puzzled look on my face, I knew Malvo could see that I didn't understand. Why would he fight a sergeant when they didn't even know each other? When I looked at the man named Bones, I could see the disdain in his eyes and had no idea why. A day ago, none of us had even met. I believed we hardly had time to make enemies, especially with men on our own side. No matter how I looked at it, it made no sense.

Everybody in the large saloon backed off, making a circle for the men to have it out. It was like reading a novel about a faraway place I'd never been to. Malvo stepped past the men holding the circle together and stared into the sergeant's eyes. He, too, wore an expressionless mask. Both men were about the same size, although the cavalry soldier wasn't missing an arm and an eye. I wondered how my friend was going to pull this one off. He usually thought things out before diving in, but this time, it looked like he'd thrown caution to the wind.

Suddenly, a grin crept onto Malvo's lips. That was when the color drained from Bone's face, and his eyes widened with worry. He suddenly realized what he was up against, and it gave him pause, but it was too late to change course. As the bets started, voices crackled with expectations. I heard the clattering of silver coins on the tables. The buzz in the room drowned nearly everything out. It became so crowded it was as though the mass of people breathed in and out and had a life of its own.

A short cheroot stub was clamped in Junior's sneer. I ground my teeth so hard that it hurt my jaw. I looked at Chito-Oti, and he was cleaning his fingernails with a knife, completely ignoring the event. Did he know something that I didn't? Gleefully drunk, Junior stifled another snicker, then continued to cheer Malvo on.

Bone's eyes snapped toward the bounty hunter, blazing like branding irons. He had read about him in the newspapers and sentenced his judgment before they met. Now, they were going to duke it out. He growled through gritted teeth.

They walked to the middle of the ring to shake hands, and no more did they break contact. Bones sucker-punched Malvo in the jaw, making him stagger backward. He rubbed his chin and spat out a gob of blood. Then he knowingly grinned. The look on his face made chills run up and down my spine. I was sure the sergeant saw it, too.

When the two men clashed, my guts twisted like a dirt devil on Main Street. After the first blow, there was no turning back until the end; however, it worked out. It was surprising when everything went deathly quietly right before the first blow. I found myself holding my breath.

"So, that's how it is, is it?" Malvo smiled again, but this time with bloodstained teeth.

Tanner followed the sucker punch with smashing, lightning-fast right jabs snapping the sergeant's neck back like a spring-loaded doll's head in a toy store. He kept the blows raining down until his opponent was on the ground. The sergeant's features were swollen and rearranged. In seconds, he was a bloody mess. The spectators broke out of their paralysis and applauded; some even laughed. Fists full of coins exchanged hands. Some had happy faces, and others had regret.

"No hard feelings, Sarge," Tanner huffed, out of breath.

Bones gritted his teeth, his eyes on his opponent's hand. The sergeant took another step backward as if the fight was over, then turned and went after Malvo in a rush, hoping to catch him off guard. He caught him on the chin again, dropping him to one knee, but the next second, he was up in a crouch as he circled the sergeant. From where I sat, things began to look serious. At first sight of that dark, flinty look Malvo had in his eyes, it gave Bones a jolt, making him stop in his tracks.

The sergeant fished his tongue around his mouth

and then spat out two broken teeth. They clattered loudly on the wooden plank floor among gasps from the spectators, each one hypnotized by the violence.

"Why don't we start this all over again? How about I give you to the count of three, two..." That was when Malvo hit him with two quick jabs, making his head snap back like a whip. Blood poured from a broken nose. The third punch hit his Adam's apple, making him drop to his knees and struggle for breath.

The searing pain seared across his face and deep into his brain, creating a line of hot fire, making his head throb with every beat. The cut on Bone's face felt like a bullwhip's popper slicing through his skin. His breath began to come in ragged gasps as he fought to remain conscious and upright. His body obeyed his demands as he struggled back to his feet. He knew he was whipped, and it was all fair and square. When he looked down, all he saw were black and blue marks across his skin.

Finally, Malvo yelled, "Whoa, now! This has gone far enough. How about we call it a draw and leave it at that? Otherwise, one of us is bound to kill the other because neither of us knows how or when to quit."

The sergeant knew that he couldn't beat Malvo on his best day and was aware that his opponent knew it, too. Despite what he said, the bounty hunter was giving him an honorable way out of an impossible situation. This way, neither one would lose face nor make any enemies.

After the fight, Sergeant Bones shook Malvo's hand like it was a water pump. He grinned, showing two missing teeth. "You're the second hardest man I've ever fought, maybe even the first. I've never seen a man punch so fast. No wonder you only need one hand."

That evening, we all sat on the porch with cigarettes and Cheroots glowing in the dark. Junior snored loudly, sleeping off the drink. The sergeant's face looked like a punching bag, and Malvo had a busted lip and cuts on his jaw. Nobody came out unscathed, but strangely enough, they seemed to make a new bond of mutual respect.

"I always said that the best way to know a man is to test him with a bare-knuckled fistfight. Some of my best friendships started like that."

Sergeant Bone looked at Malvo from the corner of his eyes and relaxed when he saw him smile. He whispered, "Thanks for lettin' me look good with my men. It wouldn't do if they didn't think I was as tough as nails."

"If you ain't tough as nails, I'm a daisy. Most men don't get more than the one punch."

After it was all said and done, I still wasn't sure what the lesson was. Or maybe there wasn't one. It was true that two men who instantly clashed had become apparent friends in record time, all due to a fight.

thirteen
company's retreat

When a man on the fort's wall-walk put his bugle to his lips and sounded the alarm, we all knew what it meant. The cavalry companies had been missing for two days as the Comanche continued on the warpath. The lieutenant had disobeyed a direct order to return to the fort, and it was now suspected that he paid the price. Everybody who had permission climbed the ladder to the top of the fort walls. They had a bull's-eye view of the landscape.

Nobody knew whether to believe the Indian lied or if the officer had run off the rails, like the Choctaw Indian had suggested. Too many of the young lieutenants sought fame rather than carefully hunting the enemy while protecting their men. Some had come this far west for the glory and nothing more, hoping to be depicted in the newspapers back east.

After the saloon fight, the missing soldiers were the focus of most of the conversation and gossip within the fort walls. Some of the missing were friends, and others were so new they had yet to know their names. All they could remember their frightened faces.

Later, when they deemed it safe enough to retrieve the bodies, the guesswork would begin. Of a hundred and twenty cavalrymen, thirty-six new recruits arrived three days before their first and possibly final mission. The ones they couldn't identify would be buried in a common grave with their names carved into a flat piece of wood. This would give their families someplace to pay their last respects if they were up to the dangerous voyage to Fort McKavett and return.

When the initial alarm was called, Lieutenant Zook volunteered to lead the two army-sized companies to scout the fort's surrounding area for signs of hostile Comanche or Apache. Word had been out that two small ranches had been hit, a hundred miles southwest of Fort McKavett. Nobody expected it to be more than the usual small war party, when in fact it was an uprising unlike anyone had seen in years.

For the time being, the only people allowed entry to the fort were the ranchers and farmers surrounding the compound, who had managed to escape with their lives. Other than them, the traffic had come to a standstill. Not even the stagecoach arrived, and the overlanders had turned back or fallen in their flight as the large bands of warriors attacked every White man they encountered.

"Just because you have a crazy notion doesn't mean that you should run off and risk getting shot all to hell," Malvo growled. "Next time you race off to save an army company, I'm gonna stop ya. In the end, you see that it was all for nothing. I know those fools ignored your warning and went chasing after something they should never have stirred up. They were no match for the sleeping beast roaming the plains. The only possibility was to fight them off from the fort and send out small patrols to strike and retreat. That or batten down the hatches and force them to keep their distance, but then all the wagons outside the fort stand to be ransacked and burned. It appears too late for Lieutenant Zook and his men."

"I didn't know you missed me that much, pard." Chito-Ochi chuckled. "And since when did you start telling me what I can and can't do? If I remember right, I'm a grown man and I make my own choices."

Malvo, Chito-Ochi, and I pulled out our spyglasses and looked to see what the Indians were up to now. Regardless of what the captain thought, we doubted they would try to attack the fort because there was no way they would get close enough to do severe damage despite their vast numbers. The log walls gave twenty feet tall cover. The men above the Comanche on the wall-walk could pick them off one at a time with their modern 1866 Winchester repeater rifles.

They also knew about the shooter with the buffalo gun who had killed their men from a distance so far that they no more than dots on the horizon. Of course, he was the one they wanted the most, but their war chief wasn't prepared to risk his men for restitution during a war. And for the Comanche Indians, that was what this was. With two hundred fifty braves fighting across the plains, it was an all-out attempt to stop the flow of White men and their families onto their land.

Unlike the Cavalry lieutenant, the Indians did their homework before they closed in. They weren't called the lords of the plains for nothing. They appeared to attack recklessly. When I paid attention, I noticed they usually retreated after losing only a few men. It was unlike their White enemy, which often fought to the last man standing. Then again, they knew what awaited them if they were to be captured. They valued their warriors and knew they were hard to replace when the United States Army had an endless supply of soldiers and weapons and could choose when and where they fought.

"Is that what I think it is out there on this side of the ridge?" I rubbed my eyes, not believing what I saw. I couldn't help but gasp. I didn't know the man I was looking at, but I recognized the fancy officer's uniform and the fact that it was covered in blood.

"It looks like the lieutenant found the Comanche war party," Chito-Ochi said dryly. "If he had listened to me, he and his men would be sitting here with us in the fort's safety. He sacrificed two companies for nothing more than his vanity. I noticed his arrogant tone when he refused to take me seriously while delivering the captain's orders. We've seen it time and again. Men like that don't last long out here in Comanche territory."

The captain stood watching in shock as he peered through his field glasses. In the distance, he saw the lieutenant sitting on a horse with his army saddle attached to a makeshift cross, holding him upright. The lieutenant's arms dangled from the wooden arms as they supported his body, so he didn't tumble off. His red skull shined in the sun as the warrior on the pony beside him shook his blond hair in his fist. There was no mistaking who it was. Riley wondered how much they tortured him for his sins.

"What do you think happened to the rest of my men, Malvo?" Captain Riley asked.

There was deep concern in his voice. He was an officer who truly cared for his men but had to deal with the officers that Washington sent him. Most of them signed up to see the Western frontier and defeat the heathens they had read about in the newspapers. They didn't understand the situation or what they were getting into. Again, arrogance proved the wrong choice, and Lieutenant Zook paid the price.

"I'd say your man there rode them to their deaths. They aren't just out there clowning around and making a show of what they've done. They're taunting us, hoping we ride out and try to save him if he's even still alive. Even if he is, I doubt he'd wanna live with no hair and a scar for life, and that is only the part we can see from here. Most men who are scalped in this heat don't survive. The Indians wouldn't let us have him anyway. Even if we managed to get that far, they would execute the lieutenant before we reached him. Of that, I had no doubt."

"We can't just sit there and let them do this to one of my officers. We must do something! My men are watching," the captain said.

"You're thinking exactly what they want you to

think," Malvo said without taking his eyes off the soldier on the ridge. "Odds are a couple hundred Comanche warriors are just over that rise waiting on a foolish patrol to ride out and bring that reckless officer in. I bet he wishes he'd listened to Chito-Ochi right about now. He made his bed, and now he's gotta sleep in it. You'd better calm down, Captain. There's nothing we can do without foolishly losing more men, which I'm bettin' you can't afford. After the loss of two companies, won't you be short of soldiers? You suffered a blow due to Zook's recklessness."

Pulling his binoculars from his saddlebags, Lieutenant Zook put his field glasses to his eyes, edging them along the long ridge in the distance.

"Whatcha see out there, Lieutenant?" The private couldn't hide the tremble in his voice. He was nearly scared to death.

He had only arrived at Fort McKavett three days before they were deployed to chase hostile Indians. He didn't even know the names of the men who rode at his side. He was another rpair of shiny boots. No one paid attention to what happened to him. For some reason, the veteran soldiers ignored all the debutant troopers. None of them wanted to make friends, knowing they might die in the following days, and getting attached made for reckless soldiering.

He had a bad feeling about the current situation. Some men had heard what the Choctaw messenger said and were alarmed. They had seen green officers make lethal mistakes in the past, and none of them wanted to die. But they didn't want to get shot in the back for desertion either, so they reluctantly followed orders. Their commanding officer obviously didn't believe that a few Indians were much of a risk. If what the messenger said was true, hundreds of warriors could be out there somewhere.

"I see the same thing as you but only bigger, Private," Zook snapped. The officer's arrogance smelled of expensive schools and rich families from back east.

"You know what I mean, sir. Are the Comanche waiting over that hill? My bet would be they are. The messenger was right. That Indian is an army scout, so why would he risk his life to lie to us?"

"I sure as hell hope that it isn't a lie. That is what we came out here to do, didn't we? Find the enemy, split them up, and drive them into the ground, eliminating every last one. I've studied these tactics repeatedly in the classroom. Now, I'll have the chance to put my studies into practice. It's about time we found a fight. I was beginning to believe the hostiles were too afraid to engage our superior forces."

When the rifle cracked, it sang through the stillness. They could hear it when it hit flesh and bone. The private's hands clawed at the wound in his neck as he dropped to his knees, struggling for his life. Much to Zook's dismay, the corporal beside him tackled the lieutenant, probably saving his life. He had seen too many reckless young officers die during the first minutes of a fight. They might be all right if they could make it through the first few of hours.

"Get your hands off me at once! Get ahold of yourself, mister! It was just a lucky shot. I wasn't in any danger. Never lay your filthy hands on me again, is that understood, Corporal?"

Several more rounds came from over the ridge, but it was clear they were wild shots. Still, more bullets came inbound, missed their marks, falling short, some ricocheted into the distance while kicking up clouds of dust. It was all designed to excite the enemy into charging or making a mistake, and then the hammer would fall.

"The captain always says that we should carefully judge what we try to tackle or not. The Comanche are wicked fierce, sir. I know you've not come face-to-face with them yet but take my word for it; we'll have our hands full if they *are* out there in the hundreds like that messenger claimed. I doubt we'll have a chance with so many new recruits."

"Why, that messenger was no more than a heathen just like them. For all we know, he was lying, and he's a Comanche spy himself. I very much doubt the captain sent us out here to return empty-handed. Now that I have the opportunity, I have no intention of letting it pass me by. This could be the opportunity of a lifetime, Corporal. Why, if we do as well as I believe, I might recommend you be promoted to sergeant, and I may well walk away with a well-deserved medal."

"Why, thank you, sir," the corporal replied without conviction. He knew the difference between a

Comanche and a Choctaw. He believed every word the messenger said. But he was in the army and required to obey orders no matter what. The officer in charge was always right. If he turned and ran, he was sure Zook would take great pleasure in shooting him in the back. He looked down his nose at all his men, bar none. Obviously, Zook didn't think much of Captain Riley either, or he would have followed his orders.

The lieutenant pulled a saber. It flashed in the sunlight as he waved it over his head and yelled, "Skirmish line, gentlemen! Hold the line, men, at a quick trot." His horse pranced in the middle of the spearhead. It was biting at the bit, like its rider, eager to engage.

Over one hundred soldiers walked their horses onto the plains like they owned the place. All the time, the lieutenant had a grin on his face. From his expression, it looked like he was living a dream. He knew that he was ready to meet his destiny and claim his fame. He had been hoping of this day all his adult life and now had the opportunity to make a reputation for himself. Some of the soldiers were hardened veterans of decades of war with the Indians, and others, like their lieutenant and the dead private, were replacements for men killed or wounded in action. The rotation in the frontiers forts was fast and furious.

"Now, where are all those dangerous Indians?" the captain taunted his corporal. "It looks like they saw us, put their tails between their legs, and ran away. And here I was, ready for a fight. Well, what are you waiting for? Let's go see if we can catch a few stragglers. CHARGE!!!"

As they rode holus-bolus for the top of the hill and whatever was waiting on the other side, it looked like they wouldn't meet any resistance at all. The officer in charge rode waving his sword, laughing as he raced his charging horse ahead of his men until he left them in the dust cloud in his wake. The men reluctantly followed. Of course, the newcomers were as enthusiastic as their lieutenant. As far as they could see, they had nothing to fear, and their superior was right.

The veteran troopers let the others recklessly race ahead as they pulled their rifles and hoped their leader was right. But deep down inside, they all knew the truth.

When a cacophony of bullets hit them from their flanks, they had caught them completely by surprise. Then, the main force came racing on horseback over the rise and into full view. The war party was so dense and wide that there was no way even to try to estimate the number of their opponents. Bullets cut through flesh and blood as horses screamed and threw their riders to the ground.

Soldiers wandered around on their horses aimlessly with their bodies full of arrows. The smell of death was everywhere they turned. In less than ten minutes, the Comanche war party of over two hundred fifty men cut through the cavalrymen like butter, leaving behind only the dead and wounded. Not a single White man remained standing. It was the slaughter the veteran soldiers had feared.

When the dust settled, the Comanche warriors counted the bodies of the dead. Miraculously, the war party had lost only two warriors, and a half-dozen more were injured. Another fell off his horse, breaking his neck. Stray rounds from one side or the other toppled a few others. They scalped the wounded, leaving them to die. There were over a hundred in all, half of them deceased, and the others wouldn't make it through the day. Some of them would have been unlucky enough to be alive, but little did they know they had been chosen to torture and question.

Some of them, more experienced cavalrymen, turned their own weapons on themselves and took their own lives. They knew what awaited those who lived to meet their captures face-to-face. Before it was over, they would be wishing that they had taken their lives, too.

The calvary officer in charge studied the Comanche leader carefully through the blood pouring down his face from his scalped head. He was still in shock, and the result of his recklessness had yet to set in. He was too dazed to think straight after the war chief gave him a taste of his tomahawk. While still mounted, he knocked off the lieutenant's hat, grabbed his blond hair in one fist, and, with a knife, removed it with the other.

The war chief's tired eyes stretched open, showing thin lines of veins and centipede-like scars covering his face. This wasn't his first battle, and none of his men were newcomers to the long war the whites perpetrated on their people. They had no illusions of what was to be done. Zook could feel his breath on his face and smell the buffalo grease on his skin. Before he knew it, he was tied to a cross. He wobbled in the saddle as his head still spun uncontrollably. Wet pigging string bound his hands and feet, and as it dried, it became tighter, cutting into his snow-white skin.

The Indians went through the soldiers' things, taking anything of value while under the great bowl of a sky. They worked in a sober silence, save the occasional war cry as another scalp was taken.

Blood puddles formed under the white bodies that littered the entire hillside. It was the massacre the war chief had planned, and the cavalry officer took the bait hook, line, and sinker. Not only had he paid the ultimate price or his arrogance, but he had also cost the lives of all his men. Lieutenant Zook realized the depth of his mistake as he took his last breath.

fourteen
outlaw town

Pedro Flores sat beneath his large sombrero as his heart hammered between his ears. It was the morning after a session of tequila with his friends in a small Pecos Cantina. Like him, his amigos were from south of the border. He spat to remove the bitter taste in his mouth, but his tongue was so dry it stuck to the roof of his mouth. His lips were chapped.

As his head spun, he wondered if a breakfast of tortillas and rice would settle his churning stomach. Did he need the hair from the dog that bit him, or would it just make him feel worse? The morning heat was beginning to swelter as beads of sweat ran down his face and brow, stinging his eyes. The early sun wavered in the distance as it began to break the horizon and rise into the sky.

When he heard the whipcracks pop in the air, he groaned and opened his throbbing eyes. What he saw suddenly made him jump to his feet and stare. A large, aging stagecoach roared past him not twenty feet away.

When he saw the driver, he had to look twice and make a retake. He instantly knew the one-armed man with one eye at the reins. He also recognized the Indian sitting beside him.

Pedro would know the man who killed his brother anyplace, even on a recklessly roaring stage surrounded by dust. The same went for the Choctaw Indian cracking the whip. Flores had sworn to kill both men. He immediately knew he had to have someone ride two hundred miles south to Outlaw Town on the Rio Grande.

It was two hundred ninety-eight miles from Pecos, Texas, to Piedras Negras on the river border with very little in between, except a small settlement of outlaws with a camp of some twenty men plus their wives and children. This was one hundred miles upriver from the nearest Mexican settlement and out of reach of the Mexican army.

The Flores Outlaw Gang rarely committed crimes in their home country. Why have the local authorities chased them when they could cross the river and, strike North American settlers and quickly escape back across the river and to safety? So far, the dreaded Texas Rangers hadn't had enough reason to ignore the borders and ride into Mexico to apprehend Flores and his men. Until then, they were considered to be more like petty thieves and rustlers than men with bounties on their heads. Maybe all this was just about to change.

In Texas, where there was gold, greedy men wanted it for themselves. Of course, Pedro had heard the same rumors that ran wild across town, but like much gossip, it didn't amount to much. This time, he had a gut feeling that what he had heard whispered in saloon corners and allies was true, and the mystery stage was probably carrying gold.

Why else would anyone hire two such bounty hunters and cross Texas without passengers or luggage across the most dangerous stretch of the state? He saw his chance to kill two birds with one stone: get rich while acquiring restitution against two of his sworn enemies, and if they did it right, the law would think the Comanche did it.

Of course, Pedro had heard about the uneasy situation with the Comanche Indians, who were just about to let their ugly heads roar. Because they lived south of the river for countless years, the Apache and Comanche ignored the Mexicans as long as they left the members of their tribes unscathed or unhindered.

Outlaw Town was built on land that nobody wanted. There was no gold or silver to be had, nor was it of any strategic value. But this made it the perfect location for an outlaw gang's hideout. It was close enough for them to reach those with money but too far away for town posses to travel, making them almost untouchable.

Pedro pushed himself up and onto wobbly legs and headed back into the cantina, where three more of his gang continued their fiesta. Diago's birthday was two days prior, when the party started. As adrenaline raced through his body, he forgot his hangover and started to plan on how to rob the stage and kill the bounty hunters guarding the gold. But first, he had to get twenty of his men together. Anyone who was sharp enough to kill his brother was a man who was to be approached with caution.

When Flores pushed his way through the batwing doors of the cantina, he saw his gang members semiconscious at the same corner table he had left them hours earlier. Shot glasses sat empty before each man, accompanied by several empty tequila and mescal bottles. All that remained at the bottom of the bottles was the larvae of the Comadia Redtenbacheri moth. Since they were still dead drunk, the boss pulled his quirt and smacked their hands and legs until they sat up, complaining, finally getting their full attention.

Pedro Flores was considered a very dangerous man, and his men knew all about it. Each one had seen exactly what he was capable of. They feared their gang leader more than they did the Comanche, and that was going some.

"Sober up, fools. We've got work to do. Juaquin, you and Diego ride south to Outlaw Town and get some men ready. We've got a job to do and some juicy loot to steal. Alejandro and I will follow the stage that just ran out of town via the south road to San Antonio. It's obvious they're trying to throw somebody off track by taking the longer route through Comanche territory. You heard the gossip. Tanner and that Choctaw Indian friend of his are taking a shipment of gold or silver to the banks in the big city, and we're gonna make sure they don't make it. They have a good string of horses, too. It's an opportunity too good to miss."

"How many of the gang do you want, Jefe?" Diego

asked. "You know they ain't gonna be happy riding across Texas in this heat and with the Comanche on the warpath."

The boss got mad when his gang members continued to moan and groan. He smacked Diego on the cheek with his quip, making him shout, "Why'd you do that, Pedro? That was uncalled for." A red welt grew on his face, and a tiny string of blood dripped off his chin. "You've got my attention. You don't have to be mean.

"Twenty men, including us, should do the trick. All we've gotta do is figure out how to stop the stage. Twenty rifles against two gunmen and whoever else is inside won't be a match for us. I heard a rumor that Marshal Boone was going, too. That just makes me all that much surer that there's gold in that coach. If not, why all the heavy artillery?"

The other two men held their heads as they throbbed. They had gone through much more liquor than their boss, but as soon as they saw there might be gold in the equation, they all perked up, their eyes spread wide.

"Barkeeper! Bring me some coffee to sober these fools up. Alejandro, you'll come with me. We'll follow the stage until you boys return with another sixteen men. We'll meet you just before Fort McKavett. How about at the watering hole twenty miles east of the settlement? That'll be far enough away from roaming cavalry patrolling the area, keeping the road to town safe."

"What about the Comanche?" Diego asked. "And

the soldiers at the fort? I heard they send out regular patrols."

"We're not gonna attack the fort, fool. We'd end up hanging from one of those great oaks outside the fort walls. Plus, they'll have their hands full shortly when the Comanche attack the settlers and farmers in the surrounding area."

"And what about Comanche War Chief Mee-Low? He's under the orders of Chief Santana and pulls some weight. I know he's getting on, but he's still full of fight. He has some of the best warriors, too. Since he led the raid across Texas, he's one of the most respected chiefs in the Comanche Nation. Despite the treaty, I don't trust him. If we give him guns, one of these days he'll probably turn around and use them on us."

"I'm hopeful our treaty will hold. Remember, it's much harder to find ammunition for an Indian than it is a gun, and they get their bullets from us. The chief's too smart to shoot himself in the foot. Especially if we promise him a case of Winchester cartridges after we steal the loot. See, that word gets to the chief before you ride back, but don't linger. These boys raced out of town hell-bent for leather. Nope, they're not gonna turn on us. We're the best source they've got. None of the chiefs will let them meddle with our agreement as long as we keep 'em happy. But they can't find out what we're after. Everybody had guns and bullets for sale if you have enough gold."

"So, how do you want to do this, Pedro?" Diego asked. "If you said the stage is big and the horses strong, we're gonna have to figure out how to slow it down or stop it."

"Let me worry about all that. You know which routes to take. If we don't break our part of the treaty with the Comanche and the Apache, we should be all right. They'll all do whatever they can to keep us supplying them with what they need. I don't care how many white men they kill. When did they do us Mexicans any favors? If I know Malvo Tanner, he'll be riding with his men armed to the teeth, so we'll have to be on our toes."

"Did you say, Malvo Tanner? Ain't he the man who killed Geraldo, your brother?" Diago asked. "Do they have any more men with them? We need to make plans. It would help if we had more intelligence. Did you get a look at who was riding shotgun inside?"

"Chito-Ochi was with him. Where you find one, you'll usually find the other. You let me work out the details. All you've gotta do is ride south with the message and get your tails back here and quick. And don't forget to have someone send up smoke signals to Chief Santana so all the Indians see it. That should keep us safe on that front, at least for now. We might not be the only outlaws after a stagecoach full of gold. I didn't believe it initially, but the rumors all over town were right. I saw the two with my own eyes. The word is the Pecos marshal is with them and a couple more fellas, but I don't know who they are. Tanner won't be riding with beginners."

"I agree; anybody riding with him has to have a set of stones. The couple of times I've seen him, he made me nervous, and he didn't even look at me. He had one hell of a reputation for killing outlaws."

"Just take it for granted that the men with them are as dangerous as Tanner and tread lightly, and we won't underestimate them. If we catch up with them at Fort McKavett, there will be plenty of time to hit them before they get to San Antonio. It's a hundred fifty miles to the city with countless places for an ambush. But I've got to devise a foolproof plan, or Tanner will smell that something isn't right."

fifteen
the killing fields

Despite our urge to get on with the journey and get back on the road, we knew we had to wait until we discovered exactly what had happened to the army companies. But before we could even do that, we had to wait until the Comanche got tired of slinging arrows over the fort's walls and into the village. A man, two women, and a child had been injured over the course of the last three days. The bunglers kept their eyes on the distance and sounded the alarm every time they saw a cloud of arrows, but it was a different story at night.

Now, everyone knew that they had to be careful when walking around the compound and between the saloons and shops in the dark. They walked on the boardwalk under the awnings and roofs or close to the side of the fort walls. Over two hundred Comanche had no shortage of arrows and lances. Every morning, a clean-up detail rushed around collecting projectiles from the ground and where they were buried into posts, walls, and even watering troughs. They had the fort surrounded and confined by the threat of death. For now, nobody was getting in, or out.

I was afraid to open my mouth because my voice would give away my nervousness, and Malvo or Chito-Ochi might hear. I was so scared I could smell the stink on my body. I had spent the last three days on the wall-walk, peering over the log walls and tracing the distance with my spyglass. But every time I looked, I saw hostile Indians just out of range. They had been there for days and gave no sign of when they might leave.

After the lieutenant died, the Comanche tied a rope around his neck and hung him from a large oak tree on a low limb where they could pierce his dead body with their lances and knives when they passed. His corpse swung to and fro in the stiff breeze. The hostiles left him there as a reminder of what they would do if someone wandered out of the fort and made a break for it. But the captain had given stringent orders: no one was to leave the safety of the fort's towering walls without his permission, civilians included. He had lost enough bodies in this Comanche uprising, and he didn't intend to lose any more.

The night before, the Indians had snuck up to the edge of the fort and set six wagons on fire. Luckily for the owners, days earlier, they were allowed to drive their wagons into the fort and unload all their valuables. However, none of the wagons, carts, and carriages, nor the animals that pulled them, would fit inside, so they had to take their chances with their means of transportation outside the walls with the hostiles.

The fort was teaming with people from farms and

ranches within a hundred miles, plus the overlanders. With so many mouths to feed, soon there would be a question of supplies. I wondered if the Indians intended to starve us out. Then, we would be forced to fight to hunt for food. Right then, I saw no end to the siege, and I believed our future looked darker every day. Still, despite my feelings, I tried not to let it show. My friends, the bounty hunters, never showed signs of concern or weakness. When I looked at them, all I saw was determination and courage, and here I was as scared stiff. Then again, I have had a dark past with the Comanche people. To me, they seemed terrifying and indestructible.

Buckets of hot grease were pulled up to the parapets and dropped on any Indians who used ropes to try to scale the walls. I could hear them scream when the boiling oil and fat hit their arms and faces, then the thud when they dropped to the ground. Even with a half-moon, the shadows were too dense to penetrate and see what had happened until the following day. But as usual, when morning came, there was no sign that they had even been there, although we knew it was true because the ropes remained. Again, in the dark of night, the Indians silently collected their wounded and dead, never leaving anyone behind.

"I can remember back when my family insisted, we go west, and I felt almost impatient. My father thought life was free for those brave enough to cross the great vastness and claim what was theirs. I dreamed of a chance at a new life where we wouldn't be as poor as church mice. The funny thing is that we almost made it. After five years, the ranch was finally about to turn a profit and a good one at that. Then my world came tumbling down to worse than when we were poor. Now that I look back, I realize that money wasn't all that important. My family was, though."

"It sounds like you had a fine ma, pa, and brother, Benji," Chito-Ochi said. "I don't know what becomes of my family, but back east, the White men aren't so hard on the working Indians. Rather than making war, we worked together and got along as best we could. Maybe my people didn't want to be as free as the Apache and the Comanche. Those that hadn't agreed to go onto reservations appeared to be ready to fight until they died and would take as many White men with them to the other side as they could."

"And what brought that on?" Malvo asked, eyeing me with questioning eyes. "Reminiscing about the past ain't healthy. Take it from a man who knows from experience. How about you, Benji? How are you holding up?"

"I don't know. Maybe I'm a little homesick, too. Don't get me wrong, I feel like you two are my family now, but I still have the memories, and sometimes I dream at night. On the brighter side, I learn something new every day from you and Chito-Ochi. It's been a long journey from there to here."

"There's hundreds of things that I don't know." Malvo grinned. "That's not counting what I've forgotten. It takes a smart fella to be a teacher but an even smarter one to be a good student. I reckon you're the best I've ever seen at learning things. Whatcha think, Chito-Ochi? The boy's smart, ain't he."

"I believe little Yellow Hair was an Indian in another life. This is why he learns the way of the Great Plains with such ease. He is like a sponge soaking up knowledge. One day, you will be a wise man, Benji Willow. I'm proud to be your friend."

Malvo lounged against the fort wall with his face close to mine with his Sharps rifle resting on the top. When we talked, we whispered.

"Why are we whispering, Malvo?"

"Indians are good with a bow and arrow, and some of the better archers can put an arrow right where a sound is. Like us standing perched on the parapet. Like I always say, all it takes is one mistake. So, we whisper so they can't tell exactly where we are."

I felt my Adam's apple bob up and down as I tried to swallow, but my mouth was suddenly too dry. If Comanche were such formidable enemies, how would we defeat them if they tossed caution to the wind and rushed the fort, two hundred fifty strong? Malvo must have seen my expression, or maybe he smelled my fear.

"Don't worry, Benji. Everything's gonna be all right." When he said it, it settled my nerves. It was so heartfelt I believed every word he said.

Suddenly, the night erupted into flashes of gunfire followed by a thunderstorm of bullets, but it was all for nothing. I didn't duck because I knew it was outgoing and not incoming. The angry and frustrated soldiers wasted their ammunition on invisible enemies. We knowingly kept our heads down as we listened to the cracks and thuds. I saw muzzle flashes up and down the line as they took things into their own hands and fired into the dark, hoping against all odds to hit something.

A hundred bullets slammed into the ground across the distance, ricocheting off rocks and stones. The smell of gun smoke filled my nostrils and burned my eyes. Even when it was over, gunshots continued to echo in my head, making my ears ring something fierce.

"What in the world are those danged fools doing wasting good ammunition shooting at cacti, rocks, and trees?" Chito-Ochi yelled. "Stop it, Captain, before they hurt themselves."

A red-tinged calm settled over me when the guns fell silent. When it started, I felt like ice was injected into my veins as a cold chill ran down my spine. All I could do was hope that the soldiers didn't break ranks and fall into the Indian's deathly trap. Still, they tried to lure us in but eventually without success. One look from their captain and the angry soldiers stopped. There were no red faces of embarrassment, like I'd expected. They had done what they did, and they owned it. I marveled at the relationship the captain had with his men.

"That'll be enough for now, boys. Calm down and put your guns away. We've wasted enough bullets for one day. Go back to your positions. We're still in siege here."

He watched some of his men take their positions on the parapet around the fort walls while the others descended and returned to their duties or one of the saloons.

"Don't worry. They won't panic again," Captain Riley assured us. "They're a bunch of soldiers—maybe even killers—but not freedom fighters, and they follow orders when it's important."

"But you hardly said a word to them for wasting all of their bullets," Marshal Boone huffed.

"You can't always lead with admonishments. Sometimes, you must let them blow off a little steam or one night, I'll find a few who have gone over the wall and struck out to get revenge on their own. Being a good leader and keeping your men alive is a complicated business, Marshal."

Despite his gruff mannerisms and tough talk, Marshal Boone had turned out to be a fine man. I was shocked that it had come to me as such a surprise. For some reason, I thought he was a devious person, not too far from an outlaw himself, like I had read about in the dime novels. I couldn't have been more wrong. Lem was usually serious except when he looked at me and smiled. I could see that it reached his eyes, and I knew that behind all that huffing and puffing was a kind and honorable man.

The captain stared at his new friend with keen interest. In the short time we were there, I could see he learned a couple of things from Malvo and maybe vice versa. Both men were big on respect, which was their most profound bond. I didn't know if we would ever return this way again, but I sure hoped so. But sometimes, when there was no Comanche around. I've seen enough war for now.

Like I'd been doing for the last few days, I slept

under the carriage on a nice bed of hay at night. I initially slept in the carriage curled up on the soft cushioned seats, but I couldn't bear Junior's snoring. It was like sleeping next to a bear.

At first, the sound came gradually. It was faint as it grew out of the darkness. Initially, it was something that I had imagined, but now I could hear the unmistakable sound of someone slowly walking. The first signs of light showed on the eastern horizon. In a few minutes, the sun would rise, bathing everything in light. When I looked up, I saw a yellow circle cast on the ground from a lantern. His legs and guns were visible, but the rest of him was in the shadows.

Then came the sound of the mournful squeak of hinges. Junior opened the stagecoach door. "Who's out there?"

"I think the Comanche warriors have ridden off," Malvo said as he raised the lantern higher, lighting up the carriage shed. "From what I could see, the large war party is gone. They must have vanished silently into the night."

I could hear everybody's interest sparked because we all sat up straighter, and those standing leaned toward Malvo to better hear what he had to say.

"Let's get out of here then," Marshal Boone replied.

"He's right, you know. This is taking longer than I thought," Malvo said. "If we don't get moving, San Antonio outlaws will hear about us and might try to rob us as we hit town. Soon, we'll have half the state of Texas on our tail. With every tick of the clock, the odds get bigger against us.

"We can take the same route I did a few days ago. On the way, we can ride with the captain to see what happened to the lieutenant's men. Maybe there's someone out there that's still alive."

The following morning, we harnessed the team of horses, put the others on string lines, and pulled the stagecoach out of the shed. The fort gates were open, and the overlanders were going out to see what remained of their possessions. Several wagons were in ashes, and one still smoldered as orange coals glowed on the burned wagon tongue. Some men and women cheered joyfully, and others cried in despair. Still, they carried on. A wake of dust followed our wagon out of the fort gates and onto the southern San Antonio-El Paso trail. Suddenly we were exposed, and I felt as naked as a jaybird out there in the open.

After riding for half a day, we saw where the killing fields were. Below a hundred circling vultures lay over a hundred uniformed dead men. To my horror, yellow beaks and long claws ripped at the corpses' flesh. A string of coyotes raced away when we rode into the terrible mess. Tens of thousands of blowflies buzzed in the air, making my ears ring. Some of the buzzards and crows had bits and pieces of their dinner in their mouths and talons.

When we pulled up, the look on the captain's face almost made me choke up and cry. I had never seen a man so devastated. His mouth hung open like he was about to say something, but the words wouldn't come. The blood drained from his face. His color matched that of the men on the ground. Something gave me the itching feeling that maybe he believed he should have been with his men when they sacrificed their lives. Right then, I realized how hard a job it must be to be a leader of so many soldiers. All these dead because of the ego of one officer. I blinked unbelievingly, looking at the devastation so deep and wide.

Without turning his head away from the slaughter, Captain Riley said in a hushed, reverent voice, "You boys, go on now. We have an unpleasant job to do here. We must make camp and bury our brothers. Collect their valuables first, Sergeant. You might as well put everything together. Many of these men are unrecognizable, so we don't even know who they are. Did you bring the roster, Corporal?"

"Yes, sir," he replied in almost a whisper. The only sound was the cawing of crows as they lined the limbs of trees and the shifting of horses' hooves.

Without another word, Chito-Ochi cracked the whip over the six-horse team heads, and they broke into motion, nervous from the smell of so much blood. Their sense of smell was one hundred times that of a human. The horses moved eagerly, wanting to get away as they broke into a run. To be honest, I felt the same. I'd never wanted to be away from a place so badly as I did that day. I believe all my friends felt the same too. Only Marshal Boone's face remained impossible to read, but his voice was listless and full of dread. Still, we all knew we had a job to finish, and there was no room for lax travelers.

"How far do we have to go, Chito-Ochi?" None of us had spoken a word after we left the slaughter, but I felt I needed to say something. The silence was driving me mad.

"We only have a hundred fifty miles to go. We make better time than most stages because we run nearly empty and have top-notch horses. We average seven to nine hours per hour in the hilly country but ten or eleven on the flats. I reckon we'll be there in two or three days if we don't run into any more trouble. The horses and us are well rested, so we can push the teams and get a good sleep at night. But out here, you just never know."

"It sounds short, but with how things have gone so far, it might be a longer ride than we hope."

I thought that first day would never end. All I could think about was the dead soldiers by the river. I had never seen anything like it and hoped never to do so again.

mad dash to the finish

As soon as we rode off the trail to the fort and onto the road, we burst into a run. Without encouragement, the horses raced to get away from the smell. As we bounced down the path, Malvo, Chito-Ochi, and I sat on the spring-loaded wooden bench seat. Junior and Lem rode inside. Shotgun barrels hung from open windows. So far, we haven't had to use the iron covers. As we neared the end of our journey, I wondered if we would have any more trouble.

We rode all day without mishap. We stopped three times to water the horse and to have something to eat. We all needed nourishment to keep running like we had been doing for days on end. An hour before sunset, we stopped. Les and I searched our parameters for firewood or chips and any signs of tracks in unusual numbers. With the Comanche uprising, few people could be found on the southern El Paso to San Antonio trail. I figured if we ran into anyone, they would be suspect and probably there to do us harm.

"Whatcha doing?" I asked my Indian friend as he appeared to be digging little holes in the point of the lead bullets of his Colt-45s. Chito-Ochi seemed to keep his balance like a bird perched on a thin limb on a windy day. He moved in the rhythm of the bouncing stage while I was slung all over, holding on for dear life.

"I'm making up a little surprise for anybody who wants to stop us before we get to San Antonio. See how I'm hollowing out a little hole to fill with that newfangled dynamite I'm sure you've heard or read about. It just went on sale in the armories this year. Malvo and I keep up to date with all the latest weapons. Now, when one of my bullets hits an outlaw, he'll get an extra bang he's not counting on."

"How big of an explosion does it make?"

"I don't know. I've never used one. But it makes sense to me. That little hole will hold just enough explosives to make a small blast. Add that to the damage inflicted by the bullet; I doubt it matters where you hit your enemy. If I hit one in the arm, I reckon it should blow it right off, and the same should happen with a leg."

Every few hours, we stopped to let the horses catch their breath, give them water, and grease the axles. The old stagecoach ran like a fine Swiss watch. When they built her, they made quality work to last a lifetime and then some. It was as solid as an oak.

"Pshaw," Junior spat a brown stream of brown juice into the dirt. "I think it's about time we start movin' a little faster. Every day we're out here with this stagecoach is another day an outlaw can get in front of us and set a trap. When we left Pecos, most of the town suspected something was up, and with the mind of an outlaw, you can take it for granted they'll have connected all the dots. By the time we left Fort McKavett, everybody knew or at least suspected what we were doin'. This old stage is like a big sign hangin' around our necks everywhere we go. You do know that outlaws and Indians alike have spies in all the settlements even if we don't see them?"

I squinted in the dim light in the shadows. It was clear that Junior had been drinking. I saw him stare at me through filmy eyes. He stood, feet spread wide, planting them so he wouldn't sway. The last of today's sunlight flashed off the metal flask sticking out of his jacket pocket. Finally, we had an eventless day. Still, I continued to shoot glances over my shoulder. In half an hour, lightning bugs flashed across the distance, and crickets chattered as coyotes howled and yapped in the dark

We were experts at making and breaking camp and did so in record time. Some of us took turns sleeping inside, and some were under the coach. It kept the wet dew off in the wee hours of the morning. As the days blurred together, the nights passed so swiftly that it felt like we hardly got a wink of sleep.

"Why are you hanging our food from that tree, Chito-Ochi?"

"To keep it away from marauding mountain lions. I've seen tracks from a big male off and on, all day long. This one looks like it is seven feet long and weighs around one hundred and fifty pounds. That's why all the caution. Usually, they steer clear of humans, but sometimes, one goes off the rails and starts killin' people because they're an easy target. This one might be getting too old to chase wild critters down, but that doesn't mean he isn't dangerous. If anything, he's more so. Keep an eye out when you're riding under trees because that's where they'll be waiting to ambush their prey."

We pulled our saddles off our horses and put them out to graze on what little grass they could find. They pulled at tufts of green grass and slid their jaws. They seemed to be at peace after the morning bloodbath. I wished I had gotten over it as fast as they did. I was still all shaken up from the dreadful sight. I've seen battles after Indian attacks, but I'd never seen a massacre, especially with all those dead White soldiers.

I wondered if they had family, and if so, would they ever find out what really happened that day? Sure, there would probably be a court-martial, but all the men responsible were dead so that it would be for nothing. I suppose they could condemn the dead for their erroneous ways, but that was of little consolation for the grieving families.

"Why are you stomping on the ground before laying out your bedroll tonight? I've seen you do that before but never thought to ask; you know, now that I'm askin' questions. Is there something I should know about?"

"I stomp the ground to plug up any holes with rattlesnakes in 'em, so they don't crawl into bed with me at night. They look for warmth when they get cold and curl up beside your belly. As the nights cool, they'll look for warmer places to sleep. Don't worry. You can bunk inside the stage with Junior tonight. Here, put these in your ears."

I had always been careful about rattlesnakes. Back on our ranch on the Red River, we had our share. Sure, we had the occasional mountain lion kill a calf or two, but I never thought about one eating a grown man. I reckon with my smaller size; I might be a tasty treat. Thinking about it made hackles rise on my neck. That night, I slept with Junior on the stage with the cotton balls Chito-Ochi gave me stuffed into my ears.

An hour before sunset, shafts of light passed through the trees like a cathedral. Then, a few minutes later, a prism of colors reached all the way across the sky. As the sun began to disappear on the western horizon, the moon rose on the opposite side of the world. Again, it was pumpkin colored. I wondered if that was a sign. The last time I saw a moon like that, bad things happened. I wasn't a superstitious person by nature, but with so many unexpected problems, I'm starting to wonder if I should be or not.

Late that night, Junior woke up with a fierce urge to take a leak. He blinked his eyes open and listened carefully to the night. Of course, he knew one of our friends would be out there standing guard. Still, it gave him pause to walk out into the dark shadows, but the urge was too great, and he couldn't wait.

The coach door hinge screeched, waking me up. I wasn't worried, though. Junior went out to relieve himself like clockwork every night. He told me it had something to do with age. He *did* seem to go more often than I did.

When the Mexican popped out of the brush, he lowered his head, dropped his shoulder, and brought up the knife. He stared hard at Junior through half-closed eyes. The first swipe sliced through the miner's defensive arm. It happened so fast that he didn't even see it coming. Then suddenly, it gushed with blood.

He wondered how the man got there without making a sound. Junior could hear his heart scream in his ears. Then Alejandro sliced him from his cheek to his mouth, laying him open like a filet. He would have cut his throat hadn't he dodged with his head. The Mexican flicked a short arch, just missing the old man's sucked-in stomach. He screamed and tried to turn and run.

When I peeked out the stagecoach window, I saw Junior looking at me, pleading—my face was long and thin with large, self-conscious eyes. My first instinct was to freeze because I was so young. But I pushed my fears away, knowing it would be too late if I didn't do something fast.

The outlaw froze when he heard the click of my Colt Walker's hammer, but it was too late. The Mexican's eyes grew wide when he saw the large-bore pistol barrels. I had two choices: either fight or watch my friend die. I pulled the trigger, shooting him in the chest, slamming him against the wooden side of the stage.

The member of the Outlaw Town gang gasped as

his legs went limp, and he slid down the side, leaving a streak of blood.

Alejandro stopped dead in his tracks as he held his hand over his heart, which stopped beating. He waited for it to start again, but it didn't come. His blind eyes stared into the twilight, millions of miles away. Stars twinkled overhead like little spies watching our every move.

Junior looked up at me, propping himself on his elbows. He struggled to one knee and said, "You'd better get me to a doctor. I don't wanna die before I get my gold to the bank. At least then I'll be able to say I was rich." His mouth hung half open as he suddenly went numb.

I sat inside the coach for the rest of the night, watching Junior, expecting him to take his last breath at any moment. Finally, my eyes began to droop, and my head nodded, my chin to my chest. Later, from somewhere far away, I thought I heard boots scrape the ground. I woke up, and when I looked up, my Indian friend gazed at me with kind eyes. When I looked back, Junior was holding his face as he blinked.

"Careful now, old friend," Chito-Oche said. "I don't see any sign of damaged vitals. I'll fix you up as good as new with a few catgut stitches. I'd say it looks worse than it really is. You were lucky Benji was there. If it hadn't been for him, you'd be dead just like that Mexican out there."

Malvo came running from out of the dark. "Is he all right? There's another set of tracks out there. You stay here and see to Junior while I go see if I can locate the second man. We won't want him to get back to the main party if they're point scouts. You take guard duty, Marshal. I'll be back as soon as I can."

"What about me? I can't stand by after they sliced Junior up. That fella cut him up good. I wanna go with you and get revenge."

"And you shot him for what he did, didn't ya? There was nothing else you could do. I know you want to busy your mind, so you don't think about all this, but you're best to me right here to help the Les guard the gold. Chito-Ochi is gonna be tied up for an hour or so. By then, I should be back. Even the marshal will slow me down. I wanna catch this fella before he gets away."

Malvo slipped his Sharps rifle from its sheath. The moon overhead created long shadows on the western side as far as I could see. Anybody could be out there lurking in the shadows. He walked out of the camp and instantly disappeared. The marshal and I looked puzzled. How could he vanish like that with such a giant moon?

Malvo weaved his horse through briar patches and around cacti, following the tracks of the other man.; he saw he had turned and was running back to warn the others. If Tanner hadn't gotten to him in time, they might have come at them that night. If they could stay hidden until morning, they would be on the road again, and the armored stage would make us a harder target. But at night, when the horses were bedded down, and some of the men were asleep, was most vulnerable moments.

Malvo sniffed the air and was surprised to note a hint of a cheroot. Maybe this outlaw wasn't as clever as he thought he was, or he was reckless beyond belief. Any Indians around would smell his presence. When he passed under a low-hanging limb of a dying oak tree, Tanner grabbed ahold and swung himself up with one arm and his rifle strapped across his back. Like a raccoon with a hound on its tail, he scrambled up to where he could see into the distance. The moon cast a silvery shadow across the country. That was when he saw the silhouette moving from shadow to shadow. At least the other Mexicans knew how to travel. Tanner prepared his Sharps and adjusted the scope until he saw him as plain as day. The gang's scout was far off, but Malvo was confident he could make the shot.

He could smell the worn wood and gun oil as he cuddled the rifle stock to his cheek; he slid a fifty-caliber round home and slipped his finger into the safety trigger with a click. Then he gently put even pressure on the firing trigger. The gun boomed, breaking the quiet of the night. A second later, the rider toppled off his horse. From a distance, it looked like he had shot him square in the back. Malvo didn't expect any more trouble from that outlaw.

pedro flores

After finding the dead bodies of Diego and Alejandro, Pedro becomes furious. He was hell-bent on killing Malvo Tanner and Chito-Ochi and the old man with them, even if he had to die trying. The problem now was that the men he sent out as scouts had been caught, and the gunmen protecting the stage knew someone was following them. Soon, they would also know how many thieves there were because the Choctaw Indian was with them. It was said he could rack a snake across a river.

When Pedro arrived, he was breathless and wheezed, his eyes full of fire. "Am I too late?"

"No, they're all still there except for Tanner. He and that Choctaw killed Alejandro and Juaquin, ya know. Another half dozen ran for home on the river when they found out it was Malvo and Chito-Ochi guarding the gold," Juaquin said. "Hell, we don't even know if that's what they're transporting."

"What else would it be, fool? When I get my hands

on those six cowards, I'm gonna hang the bunch. How dare they run off on me when we're north of the border."

"We have nearly half the men we had yesterday, and now they know we're dogging their trail, so it's going to be harder than ever. We already missed the element of surprise because of that damned Indian and his snoopy ways."

The Mexicans from Outlaw Town huddled in a group with greedy eyes. They were like feral dogs, and their clothing were filthy. It looked and smelled like they hadn't bathed in a year. Their mismatched rags told part of their story. Remnants of soldiers' uniforms were mixed with those of cowboys and fancy embroidered jackets from Mexico City—probably things they had taken off dead bodies.

As the boss laid out a plan, Flores smiled wolfishly and then wrapped his fists around his pistol grips. His expression was cocky and cruel. He shot evil glances at each of his men as a warning. If he saw anyone running away again, they were sure to get a bullet in their back. The men who were already on their way to Outlaw Town would be served justice when he got home. If he let such things slide soon, men would want to take his place, so he had to nip it in the bud. The only way to govern a place as rough as Outlaw Town was to be ruthless and fast like a rattlesnake.

"You bunch are about as useful as a two-legged donkey," Pedro spat. "Why didn't you wait until I got here like I told you to? Now, see the fine mess you've left us in, not to mention the dead men. And how did you let part of our men run off, Diego? You're supposed to be the boss while I'm gone."

"There's always more where they came from," Diego replied lazily. "Why, most men would ride with you for free, boss."

Flores shook his head, adding, "That's why you're not the gang leader, fool." Still, he noted the compliment. One of his weak points was that he liked to be flattered even when he didn't deserve it.

"The ones that ran couldn't beat a fat man to a pie-eating contest and ain't worth the time of day," Diego said in English he learned from his American mother. His Apache father had killed her a few years after he was born. Then, he was abandoned and ended up living in Outlaw Town. The rest was the natural course of the nature of a dishonest man.

Diego was past forty, with a thin, wizened face. When he removed his cover, it showed a widow's peak. His hatband left a mark on his brow, and concern was etched across his face.

"Good men this far south and west are as rare as hen's teeth," Pedro spat. "We'll have to do with what we've got."

The whole room froze when Chito-Oche softly called out, "Don't move," as he saw Flores's face with widespread eyes. "Drop your guns real slow, like cold molasses. Mind you now, I have a nervous trigger finger."

Everyone went silent for a moment. The Indian laughed to fill the void, but it didn't ease the tension. It just showed them who was in charge.

Suddenly, the amusement in his eyes was gone, and his mouth tightened. Pedro nodded with knowing eyes. He wasn't going to walk away from all this. This would be his last mistake.

"Where the hell did you all come from?" Pedro asked. "Grab your horses, boys, and run!"

Three shots rang out, and three men fell to the ground. Smoke squirreled out of three barrels. The smell of cordite lingered in the air.

From the stagecoach, I heard the gunshots. I stood there with my gun in my hands, but I didn't know what to do. Everything happened so fast; it was over before I reacted. Junior was unconscious, and the marshal was sitting on the bench seat on top with a ten-gauge scatter gun in his white-knuckled fists. His eyes were no more than slits.

I heard the hammering hooves before I saw the riders. It was Malvo and Chito-Ochi, waving at us to jump on board. In seconds, the coach lurched into motion, and we were off at a run. Whipcracks cut through the hot air, making the six-horse team run faster.

"They're behind us!" Malvo shouted as he looked over his shoulder. "Grab the reins, Benji. I need my hand free to shoot. Back down into the steel box, we made to drive the horses from safety. Chito-Ochi, you and I can get inside and close the cast-iron windows. We can prop them open just enough to shoot. Whatever you do, Benji, keep this stage running straight down the trail. We're gonna have to fire from on the run."

I grabbed the reins in my fists. Suddenly, I felt like a little teenager doing a big man's job, but I bit my lower lip and crawled backward until only my head, hands, and reins showed. They couldn't get a shot off at me if they weren't coming directly toward us from the front. I knew they couldn't get to my friends in the back. Now, all I had to do was hold on for dear life.

The riders had no trouble catching up with the stage. Even with such a team of horses, they still had to pull all that weight. The Jinetes behind us rode like they were born in their saddles. Soon, I began to hear bullets ring and zing through the air as they hit the potbelly stove's doors and ricocheted off to somewhere out of sight. They didn't even dent the iron window covers.

Chito-Ochi took careful aim at the man beside him, who he took as the leader, just because of the quality of his horse and fancy boots with silver spurs. He had to be the one in charge. When he took his first shot, he got the surprise of his life. When the dynamite-filled round hit the outlaw's chest, it blew a hole in him the size of a water bucket, and it injured the horse, too. It went careening into another, making them both tumble to the ground, breaking its leg and the rider's neck.

Malvo turned and asked, "What in the world was that? Did you put explosives in those bullets?"

But Chito-Ochi didn't reply. He was focused on the man on the other side of the gang leader. He assumed that the best men would stick to their leader like glue. A second round exploded, making ten times the noise than a normal gun blast. This one hit an outlaw's leg, blowing it off and leaving a gaping wound on the horse's side. Both man and rider fell, dying to the ground. Even though the rider was only hit, he went into shock and bled out in seconds.

Two riders pulled to a sliding stop and tried to wheel around and run, but the leader turned and shot them both in the back. The outlaw's numbers continued to dwindle, but not a bullet one even scratched any of us guarding the stage. We were too well prepared for a wayward outlaw gang from south of the border to stop us.

As I slapped the reins across the horses' backs, I saw a narrow-hipped man with large hands and broad shoulders under a brown face with a hooked nose. When his eyes met mine, they were as black as coal and void of feeling. Somehow, I knew he was the leader of the Mexican outlaw gang. He took aim, but I ducked behind the steel plates, and the bullet sang off into the air, missing my head but inches.

"Pull the wagon to a stop, Benji, and let's finish this!" Malvo shouted.

To be honest, I was surprised because I thought we were doing a good job of warding them off without stopping and taking them on man-to-man. It was true that someone who looked like the leader had gotten a shot off at me. Save the armor; I'd be dead. Maybe Malvo had seen enough and wanted to end things once and for all before one of his friends was shot and killed.

As soon as the outlaws saw the stage pulling to a stop, they wrestled their horses into a walk and dropped down to take what wasn't theirs. Junior's gold was what they were after, but now there was revenge in their eyes, too.

Pedro Fores stood square in the middle of the El Paso-San Antonio Trail. His hands dangled dangerously close to his guns as he wiggled his fingers. He planted his feet wide as his eyes blinked. It was evident that he was beyond angry and had gone to that dark place where men live or die. He had crossed the line of no return and knew it.

I backed away from Flores's vehement words. Sure, he spoke in Spanish, and I didn't understand what he said, but his meaning was clear. I didn't need a translator to know that. To him, I must have looked like a frightened animal cowering in the corner with nowhere to escape.

Malvo kicked the stage door open and dropped to the ground.

"Who's that?" he asked with a ring of suspicion in his voice. Squinting, he studied the riders on horses. Just like Chito-Ochi said, there were originally about twenty in all, he saw from the tracks, but now, there were only three, including the leader.

"I don't know. Some Mexican outlaw gang heard about the gold and wanted it for themselves." Malvo fingered his Navy Colt.

Suddenly Tanner went for his pistol, cocking the hammer. The Mexican nearest heard the metallic click, making his head swing to the source just before he was shot. His eyes instantly went blank. Chito-Ochi fired a dynamite-filled round at two men standing together. He aimed for where their elbows touched. The dynamite-charged bullet exploded, severing both arms. They screamed in pain. When the Indian pointed his pistol at the last man standing, Pedro Flores stood there in shock. He opened and closed his mouth like he was talking, but no sound came out.

The friendliness in Malvo's voice disappeared as it turned coldly polite. "So, that's how you want it, do ya? Why, I'll be happy to oblige." He grabbed Pedro Flores by the scruff of his neck and hammered him once, twice, then a third time. Every time he stopped beating on him, he would catch his breath and drive his fists into his face again. When he was done, his knuckles were dark and bloody.

Right before we pulled the stagecoach onto the trail again, we heard the sound of squeaking rope against a tree branch. It was tied to a limb and the end to a man's neck as his dead body swung in the wind. Pedro Flore's career had dramatically come to an end.

eighteen
san antonio, texas

Malvo pushed his gun belt lower on his hip as he tightened the buckle. He was ready to go to work. He propped up against the porch post with his Winchester rifle leaning on the railing.

Behind him, he heard the screen door close softly, and then Chito-Ochi was standing at his side. His shotgun was in the crook of his arm, and his pistols were in his wide leather belt. They eyed the darkness around the stagecoach, which they had pushed into the Butterfield Station barn. Another silhouette came from around the back.

"Who goes there?" Malvo asked as he drew his Navy Colt.

"Don't shoot, it's me, Marshal Boone."

"Let's grab some hay bales from the stables and stack them three high and two deep to give us better cover. I doubt anyone else after this gold will miss their last opportunity to steal what we've got. The bad guys won't give up until they're all dead. Only the yellow ore makes men so crazy."

As I sat inside the stage, I waited with my Colt Walker in both hands. When I cocked the hammer, the click seemed loud, making me paranoid. If any more outlaws made it this far, I planned to pull the trigger until my pistol was empty. We made it to San Antonio, but the money wasn't in the bank yet, and until it was, we were all on high alert, especially on the outskirts of a city of twenty thousand people.

An orange streak showed on the eastern horizon. The sky was no longer completely dark. That was when Malvo and Chito-Och began to see shadows moving in the growing light. It was the outline of shapes of men. Suddenly, the staccato of bullets filled the stagecoach yard. They whined by, thudding into the bales of hay. Others hit the stone building behind them, ricocheting off the walls.

I was afraid to open my mouth because my voice would give me away. I was so scared I could smell it, musky and damp. I had to take a deep breath to calm my nerves.

I carried Junior inside and eased him down to the doctor's bed. When the physician lit the lamp beside him, I gasped. Junior was hardly recognizable. There was no color to his skin; his face was limp and damp with sweat, leaving his hair matted to his head.

When a girl named Darlene came in with a water basin, she mopped his face, washing away the blood. She carefully dabbed the wet towel on his eyes. When she got the broken tissue cleared, she saw his right eye was foggy, his nose broken, and he had a deep cut across his face, but the good news was he would live. He tried to push himself onto his elbows, then fell back as the lines on his face tightened from the pain.

"Benji?"

"I'm here, Junior. You can count on me and..." I raised my eyebrows at the beautiful young girl's face. She smiled at me like we had known each other for years.

"Darlene," she said before her neck went red with embarrassment, and she realized how she was acting. She couldn't have been more than sixteen, and I was tall for my age, so maybe she thought I was as old as her. I knew that most girls didn't go for younger guys.

I whispered, "Not today, Junior. We're safe now. Get some sleep, and we can talk in the morning. Don't worry about the stage. It's in the Butterfield Coach stables, and Malvo, Chito-Ochi, and Marshal Boone are guarding it. They won't let anyone get by and steal it. As soon as you feel you can walk, we'll take your belongings to the bank. We need you in shape to sign to open your account."

"Virgin Mary and Mother," Darlene gasped. "Who would beat an elderly man like this? Did you save Junior, Benji?" Her eyes twinkled when they locked with mine.

"Me and my friends did. He took a hard beating from the Pedro Fores gang, but I think he'll be all right. Do you work for Dr. Fullman?"

"Yes, I'm his assistant. I want to become a nurse. Do you work for Mr. Junior?"

"I reckon I do until our job is done."

"And what job is that?"

"To bring him and his belongings from Pecos to San Antonio in one piece."

"It doesn't look like you and your friends did a very good job."

"He's alive, isn't he? You would understand if you knew all we went through to get from Pecos to here. Just ask my friends."

There was something about this beautiful young woman that I couldn't put my finger on, but then I suddenly realized this was the first time I had felt attracted to a girl.

Junior motioned his hand for me to come near. I had to put my ear to his mouth to hear; he was so weak. "It was *you* who saved me, son. Nobody can ever take that from you, and I'll be forever in your debt."

I didn't reply because I wasn't that kind of fella. Still, I felt my face reddening with embarrassment, and I didn't even know why. Despite the whisper, I was sure Darlene had heard what he said.

"I'm gonna have to leave you now, Junior. It looks like you're in capable hands, though. I've got to help Malvo and Chito-Ochi guard your valuables."

When I got back to my friends, the town law hooked his thumbs behind his suspender straps and looked at Malvo and Chito-Ochi questioningly. He angrily stared at the dead men on the ground. After a moment, a snarl appeared on his lips. I stood to the side, and he didn't notice me when my hand neared my gun.

"You all are responsible for all this," Sheriff William Egan spat. "I'll have you two behind bars for this."

"Why, you, lyin' dirty rat!" I spat as my eyes shot daggers at the San Antonio lawman. He was as bent as a dog's hind leg,

I lost it for a moment and drove my fist into the sheriff's jaw. He staggered from the blow but didn't go down like I had planned. I should have hit him with my gun barrel. After the arduous task of blazing the dangerous trail from El Paso to San Antonio, I had enough courage to take on anything. But I was too light to knock down a full-grown man. Then his fist hit me like the hot kiss at the end of a sledgehammer, and down I went. The sheriff's voice was full of gruff challenges. At least, it was when he was talking to me. He threatened me that if I got up, he would put me down for good.

Sheriff Egan sneered with disdain at Malvo, his Indian friend, and maybe even me, but he hated Malvo the most.

Sheriff Egan was instantly rewarded with a series of lightning-swift punches from Chito-Ochi's massive fists, knocking the politician to the ground. "If you know what's good for you, *you'll* stay down," the Indian said dryly. When the sheriff pushed himself to his hands and knees while swearing at Tanner, Chito-Ochi gave him a swift kick in the gut to shut him up. "You lay your hands on that boy again, and I'll kill you." The Indian stared at him with black eyes.

"You must be one of those deaf politicians, Sheriff," Malvo said. "I told you to stay down."

"There's only one rule in this jungle. When the Lion is hungry, he eats!" the Choctaw growled, and then he spat a brown stream of juice onto the crooked lawman's head. "You're lucky we don't kill you right here and now. You know you deserved it, for sicking those fool Crowders on our tails. I would have thought you'd know better than. Now, you've left us in a predicament. Should w kill you here and now or somehow let you live? Whatcha think, Sheriff Egan? Are you ready to meet your maker?"

"But be forewarned," Malvo growled. "All the pertinent information on your false accusations and ties with the Crowder Outlaw Gang will be passed on to the army colonel here in town. Your days are counted, mister. If I were you, I'd get out of town before the marshals show up at your door. The law from Pecos has all the details."

The San Antonio sheriff's eyes watered as he spoke, and his throat choked, but I could see the relief on his face when Malvo said he wasn't going to kill him. That and he had better leave town and maybe even the state. He knew people in New Mexico where he could get a job. The only problem was that there was more lawlessness than even in Texas. Then again, he crossed that gray line of the law and went onto the other side, and had hardly noticed.

Tanner dropped his hand to his hip, brushing his coat aside and showing his Navy Colt revolver in its holster. He eyed the corrupt sheriff before him.

"If you want, we can settle this right here and now like grown men," Malvo said, drumming his fingers on his walnut grip as he waited. The sheriff slowly pulled his gun from its holster with two fingers and carefully laid it on the ground.

"I don't wanna die, Tanner. I know you'll kill me just like you did my brother."

"If you don't wanna join him in the town cemetery, it's best you be on your way. That's one thing that I can promise fellas like you," Malvo said with narrow eyes. "If you steal somethin' from me and don't surrender, you die. But if you cross me again with another trap like those wanted posters, I'll put you in the ground just the same."

The following day, we met again with Junior. He was feeling better, so we accompanied him to make his deposit. Once all the gold had been safely placed in the San Antonio National Bank, I signed a relief. It totaled fifty-three thousand five hundred dollars and fifty cents. To my utter surprise, Junior gave us a thousand dollars each.

My eyes swelled at the extravagant notion. I never imagined that I would have a thousand dollars in gold coins. Junior's generosity left me in shock.

"Don't look so guilty, Benji." Malvo chuckled. "We all earned every penny of it, remember."

"We sure as hell did." Marshal Lem Boone grinned. "Every single penny and then some."

Later that same day, I sat in a wicker chair near the saloon door. I was daydreaming of what I would do with so much money. Most of it went into a bank account that I opened under my own name. It made me feel special. I heard footsteps approaching, but I didn't lift my head. "Who is it?" I asked when I felt someone was waiting just outside the door.

A girl's voice replied, "It's me."

I looked up and smiled. "That's swell that you came. I wanted to see you before we left. I'm not gonna get to stay much longer because my boss, Malvo, says we've got a new job with the army. But when we're done, we'll be coming back to San Antonio to get paid, so I'll see you then."

Suddenly, I was out of the chair, heading for the screen door. I opened it, spilling light onto the floor. When I saw her standing there, I gasped and forgot to breathe. It made her laugh, which made me smile despite my embarrassment.

She wrapped her arms around me like she would never let go. I held her back at arm's length and looked at her up and down. She was the prettiest girl I'd ever seen. Then we embraced. It wasn't for a long time because we both felt odd and a little uncomfortable. It was the first time I'd ever hugged a girl. I already missed her and couldn't wait until we returned to spend another week or so in San Antonio. Sometimes, living in the big city was nice instead of roughing it in the wild.

When I looked down, I saw her little bosoms beginning to fill her shirt. I looked up and into her eyes, and then I had to turn away in embarrassment. My face flushed red. Finally, she chuckled, looking full of life. "Don't be embarrassed. If you didn't look at me like that, I would have thought you didn't like me. When you get back, we'll get to know each other better, and I can introduce you to my parents."

Darlene suddenly got nervous and looked like a doe ready to bolt and run. She reached over and gave me a peck on the cheek, then turned and ran off, losing herself in the dense city crowd. I touched my face where she kissed me and marveled. I had never been kissed by a girl before.

a look at:
To Hell and Back

They ran from a war...now they're running for their lives.

In the lawless shadows of a dying Civil War, Jed Coal and John Noland desert Quantrill's Raiders, fleeing through the chaos of Kansas with the Union Army, Confederate diehards, and U.S. Marshals hot on their trail. With infamous outlaws like Frank and Jesse James in their past and blood on their hands, they know there's no going back.

Jodi Goodnight, niece of legendary Texan rancher Charles Goodnight, never planned to be an outlaw. But one pistol-whipped sheriff later, she's branded a fugitive. When she crosses paths with the brooding, battle-hardened Jed Coal, the fuse is lit—on a romance neither of them asked for and a war they can't escape.

Bound by violence, driven by desperation, and hunted by every badge in the West, the trio must fight not just for freedom, but to stay human in a world that's already written them off as dead.

Will they go down in a blaze of gunfire—or rewrite their destinies on their own terms?

AVAILABLE NOW

about the author

Born in 1886 in Southern Ohio, Ash Lingam grew crops, raised cattle, and doted on the young boy. Ash's family was among the early settlers in pre-Revolutionary America. He has traced his lineage back to around 1746 when his ancestors immigrated from Europe to the aspiring American Colonies.

A retired marketing executive, Ash devotes his spare time to training police dogs and writing novels. He has found his niche in the Western, historical fiction, and adventure genres. With his vast vault of experience, he never runs out of sources for new stories. He has lived in eleven different countries and worked in a total of forty-six to date, Ash has written approximately 130 novels, short stories, and poems. More than one hundred of his eclectic titles help the American frontier come alive for his readers.

https://www.ashlingam.com/

9 781965 596500